# An Illusion of Victory

For
Andrew Carraway
Good Luck on your Big League Journey
Bobby Dews
Atlanta Braves

## Bobby Dews

**PUBLISHED BY**
Five Points Press
Athens, Georgia

1st printing, 2008
**ISBN:** 9781440453946

**BOOK LAYOUT AND
COVER DESIGN BY**
Ruffin Gillican, LLC
ruffingillican.com

# A Special Thanks

Alexine B. Dews
Marian Anne Dews
Margery Killingsworth Dews
Catherine Dews Jenkins

# AN ILLUSION OF VICTORY

## *Introduction*

After maybe twenty years of writing fiction and a little poetry from time to time, I'd just about decided I wasn't as good as I'd predicted. My time seemed to have arrived—to give up the literary dream. I was beginning to think my grandfather had been correct. I should have studied law.

So that's where I was in my thinking when Mrs. Slaton's daughter stopped me in front of the post office and said her mother, well into her nineties, some guessed older, was nearing a peaceful demise in the nursing home. There could be no doubt about the peaceful aspect. A grand lady of pure tolerance, who had taught in segregated and integrated schools, Miss Lila, as she was known around town, had requested a poem I'd written about her be read at her funeral, if in fact she turned out to be mortal. Some were beginning to wonder about this eternal citizen of Edison, Georgia.

Of course I felt honored and touched by this news. The poem to be read as eulogy was Slaton's Secret, from *Edisontown*, a modest regional book about certain people, role models, who'd made a difference in our town, people rarely making headlines, but seemingly always there when needed, living examples of lives lived with purpose and dignity.

Miss Lila was mortal and the poem was read as she passed to Heaven and we feel certain she's loved and respected there as much as she was here in the Deep South where she became the ultimate measure of tolerance, which is of course the true rock foundation for all friendship and all love.

As you would expect, the entire experience of Miss Lila's request changed my mind about the writing life, at the least, my writing life. I discovered through the life of a kind little black lady what Ernest Hemingway had discovered years ago, "Books should be about people you know, that you love and hate, not about people you study up about." And more importantly personally, "The only reward is that which is within ourselves."

Thank you Miss Lila for your gift.

*Notes*

# Title Review

*The title for this collection was created from a spell-casting passage from William Faulkner's* The Sound and The Fury. *Some consider the paragraph Faulkner's greatest writing even when taken out of context. Others consider it the greatest writing—ever. But consider it yourself.*

===================================================

# June Second, 1910

When the shadow of the sash appeared on the curtains it was between seven and eight o'clock and then I was in time again, hearing the watch. It was Grandfather's and when Father gave it to me he said I give you the mausoleum of all hope and desire; it's rather excruciatingly apt that you will use it to gain the reducto absurdum of all human experience which can fit your individual needs no better than it fitted his or his father's. I give it to you not that you may remember time, but that you will forget it now and then for a moment and not spend all your breath trying to conquer it. Because no battle is ever won he said. They are not even fought. The field only reveals to man his own folly and despair; and victory is an illusion of philosophers and fools.

**William Faulkner**
*The Sound and the Fury*
Originally Published—1929
Harrison Smith and Jonathan Cape

# BACK IN
# THE DAY
# BASEBALL

*Notes*

# A DIFFERENT GAME

My dad was fifteen when he left home to seek his fortune. One more year at Albany High and he would have had a football scholarship to the University of Georgia—so the story goes—but like many kids of the Great Depression, he couldn't wait. He ended up a journeyman minor league baseball player who also managed to serve during two wars, Korea and Vietnam, between baseball assignments in places such as Montreal, Fort Worth, Mobile and Atlanta.

Once he got the golden call, as he called it—the Brooklyn Dodgers. He phoned home before boarding an overnight train in Kansas City. He was getting pretty old, maybe this was the last chance, the only chance. But that night on the phone he sounded young, proud, ready to go. About two days later he arrived in Brooklyn and realized the dream as he anxiously pulled on a white flannel uniform with Dodgers scripted blue across the front. He told me he scorched the ball during batting practice and Charlie Dressen, the manager, assured him he'd be catching the next afternoon. It didn't happen. Brooklyn was in a tight race and my dad merely insurance if a big, long-rumored, trade died before the deadline.

The phone rang at midnight. My dad admitted he thought at first it was only a cruel prank, but soon realized Dressen was on the line and he wasn't joking. They'd made a trade with Atlanta for another catcher, a catcher that hit with power from the left side. The next day dad was back on a train, heading south.

At that time, the early forties, being an Atlanta Cracker wasn't all that bad. The pay was great, there were actually some players making as much as major leaguers, and if you were from the south anyway, it was almost like being a big leaguer. Atlanta was a teeming baseball city and the life was good. I was young, but I remember every night as a sellout and I think we won every home game and the players were treated like royalty anywhere near old Ponce de Leon Park. My mother was pretty and my dad was handsome and could hit and throw and life was beautiful. Before the games I got to play catch with the players—some nights out in front of the dugout, some nights even after they turned on the lights. Later, when I joined my mother and sister in the stands, fans would come around and jokingly ask for my

*Notes*

autograph. There was no doubt in my young mind as to my destiny.

But a five year old could only see the excitement and the beauty: the multi-tiered fences in front of the railroad tracks in right field where Bob Montag would in later years set a record for homers as he drove so many far past the lights into the darkness; or where Chuck Tanner would climb the wall like Spiderman to rob opposing hitters of many extra base hits; or the magnificent magnolia tree high upon the magnificent green knoll in center which legendary Hall of Fame slugger Eddie Mathews would bombard with gigantic home runs about twice a week.

And the smell of the popcorn, the fantastic cool thrill of a bottled Coke fresh off the crushed ice, and the feeling of pride as we waited for dad outside the locker room in the thickness of those humid Georgia nights. Then the walk home, yes, we lived that close to the ballpark. Later, as a family, we'd sit on the screened porch of our apartment and maybe enjoy a midnight snack as we listened to dad unwind as he talked about the game. There were some nights my parents let me sleep on the porch and I'd fall asleep with the glow of the lights from the ballpark on my face while listening to the late-night traffic along Ponce de Leon Avenue. And if I awakened in the night, and the lights from the field had been cut off, I was still not alone. The neon-red Sears, Roebuck sign from the south side of the street still cast a comforting light on the ballpark—the ballpark where I thought my dad would play forever.

That year my thoughts were good and clean and comforting. I didn't know about war, racism, divorce, financial problems or loneliness. God shelters the very young and the very old. And now I have been both.

My dad got drafted and our lives changed. In time, my mother and father divorced and I soon found myself living in southwest Georgia with my grandparents, while my mother and sister moved back to mother's hometown, Clinton, Iowa, where dad first met her very early in his career. They'd been eighteen and in love, having no idea how to handle what the hard war years would bring. Like my grandmother once said, "They didn't fall out of love, they just could never get together again."

In the fifties, while at Georgia Tech, my teammates and I would often attend games at Ponce de Leon Park. The Crackers were still AA, and still winning almost every game and, to tell you the truth, it was the most exciting place to watch a game I've ever known. Once in a while my buddies would look over and think I was crying and rib me a little bit. But that was okay. They just didn't understand. We weren't watching the same game.

**Bobby Dews,** *Atlanta Braves, 2005*

# APPROACHING DODD COUNTY

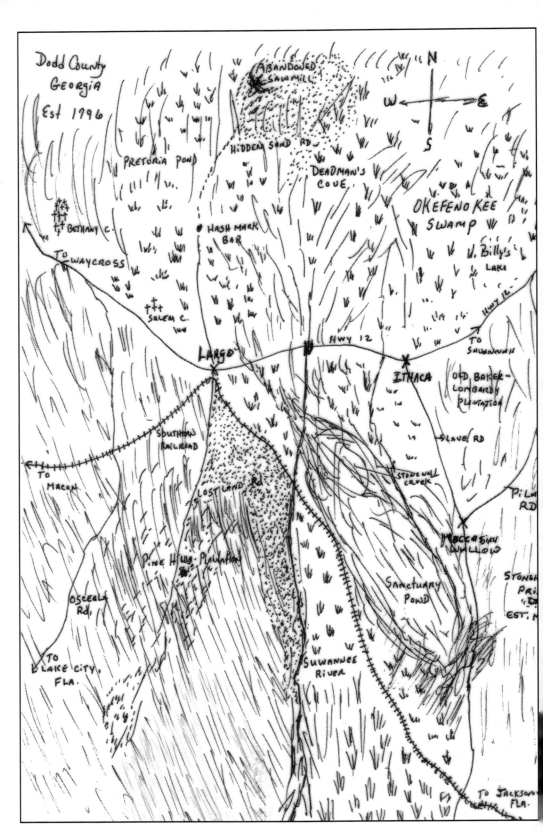

# APPROACHING DODD COUNTY

The village isn't that inferior. Granted it's dull now and then, but aren't most small towns? The number one sponsors this dullness in Largo: one bank, one law officer, one attorney, one grocery store, one bar and yes the list continues for a while and only the religious seemed to have escaped this one syndrome. No, there are not two Gods, just two churches. On the western edge of Largo, if you happen to need sanctuary, you'll find the Ebeneezer Baptist Church, while on the opposite side of town, nearer the swamp, is the Methodist Church. They say the geographic spread between the two was not meant to be symbolic. Nevertheless, the two congregations have had some differences over the years and although they adhere to slightly different doctrines, their members eventually meet in the same place. That would be Salem Cemetery. Bethany, out near Pretoria Pond, was condemned long ago.

As you see, there isn't much competition in Largo even if it is the largest town in Dodd County. Each person has a niche to fill and most citizens would be surprised if anyone strayed from these tacitly appointed roles. Most try to live within the subtle sociological framework. It's comfortable, you see. As always, some succeed and some fail, but most wallow miserably somewhere in between—except for Snakeman.

Snakeman has been eighty five for at least the past twenty years. He makes it very clear should anyone ask his age. Somehow he got it stuck in his head that if you were fortunate enough to reach a hundred—or unfortunate enough—you automatically died before your next birthday. When people scoffed, Snakeman had a way of spreading his arms (arm, really, Snakeman claims he lost his left arm to the saber of a Northern cavalry officer during the Battle Of Savannah when he was twelve and a Confederate drummer boy) which said plainly enough, "It works for me." On other subjects, as you might imagine, he was rather sketchy. But he remains somewhat a celebrity-like figure in the county, being Dodd County's only survivor of The War of Northern Aggression, as the conflict is still known in all regions of Georgia south of Macon, but not so north of Macon where they

*Notes*

play their cards somewhat closer to the vest.

Mr. Slim Benton, owner or co-owner of just about everything commercial in Dodd County, said Snakeman was full of you know what and that the old man actually lost his arm to a John Deere corn harvester way on back there before Snakeman outlived all his family. Most people disagreed with Mr. Slim and believed this to be a fabrication only to get back at Snakeman because of the conversation Snakeman had had with a Bible salesman some thirty years ago. The conversation should have made Mr. Carl "Cappy" Thorpe angry too, but it didn't, probably because Mr. Cappy was a self-proclaimed war hero, officer and gentleman of the Lafayette Escadrille, who'd flown against the Red Baron and said he actually enjoyed a glass of wine with the Baron after the German aviator forced him down following a spectacular dogfight a thousand feet between the clouds above Verdun, France.

Mr. Sid Loring, world-class checker player and retired railroad worker, made it plain he didn't believe this particular story and that he believed fifty percent of the people of Dodd County thought Cappy Thorpe lied from time to time. Mr. Cappy laughed this off, also, and said at least that rating was better than the president's recent rating and that Mr. Loring was showing definite signs of "non compos mentis." Mr. Cappy threw a lot of Latin terms around since he'd passed the Georgia Bar after attending Harvard for only one year, at least that's what he put on the application for the bar exam.

If the controversial conversation between Snakeman and the Bible sales-man did take place it took place in front of the higher-than-a-basketball-goal gray, concrete statue of a Confederate soldier in the center of downtown Largo where Snakeman could be found most of the time. According to legend, the Bible salesman had politely inquired where he might find the House of God, and Snakeman had said, while pointing with the stump of his left arm, "Well, down there that's Mr. Slim Benton's church." He looked east, "that one is Miss Arguetta's."

The Bible salesman smiled. "I see, guess that leaves God out of luck 'round here."

Snakeman smiled, showing a vast dark cavern with one tooth a stalagmite, the other a stalactite, and said rather succinctly considering the amount of vodka he invariably consumed for breakfast, "Nossir, I think God owns Sweetfield." Now he pointed the wrinkled stump west.

"Sweetfield?"

"Yessir, Sweetfield the colored folks' church 'bout five miles toward Ithaca and Moccasin Wallow—I'm fairly certain it's God's."

Everybody tended to believe Snakeman's version, after all, he was popular

*Notes*

because of the arm he'd given up defending Savannah and also because of his ability to walk past a house or business and whistle out snakes from the bushes or basements. Then like some pied piper he'd lead the reptiles back to the swamp as they followed his whistling. Most folks gave Snakeman a free meal (or beer) and others paid as much as five dollars for this service. Some, trying to cut financial corners, attempted to imitate Snakeman's weird tune, but were unsuccessful. That's why it paid to be nice to old Snakeman, especially if you lived near the swamp.

As you've noticed, Dodd County holds a bizarre, strange beckoning and since you are in the area, perhaps proper directions are in order. After you leave Waycross traveling south, the highway narrows and becomes tunnel-like beneath the ancient oaks obscuring the afternoon sun. Some motorists have even been known to switch on their headlights. It really isn't necessary, yet, for soon the road breaks into the sun as the terrain opens into a sea of thick, long saw grass and scattered pines. During the winter and then spring rains black water sulks halfway up the stalks of grass and prepares a perfect breeding spot for mosquitoes and other blood-sucking insects. During the ensuing summer drought the water slinks back into meandering channels soon too low to harbor fish and the mud banks are eventually littered with thousands of carcasses rotting in the almost tropical, relentless sun. Then, on certain nights, the wind strays far inland and the stench of dead fish and the unmistakable odor of the paper mills can be detected as far as fifty miles to the west. But after a few rainy months, fish miraculously return to the dark waters. Some old timers say the fish burrowed in the mud and survived, other older old timers say God answered their prayers and dropped the fish within the August and September harsh thunderstorms assaulting the coast after spinning from the inevitable hurricanes working their deadly ways up from the warm waters of the Caribbean. And it doesn't matter who's right. There always seem to be enough fish for everyone.

For twelve more miles the saw grass, waving indolently in a soft breeze, dominates the view; then there is a subtle slope to the land. Here you should take a look behind you at the ocean of golden grass dissected by black water canals running tortuously for a hundred miles only to seemingly end where they began. At this time of the day, the fading sun low on the savanna, the water appears navy blue and the slender pine tree trunks red as sap pops from beneath the cooling bark and oozes onto the water, sliding slick with a faint current and the wind dying into the night.

The tunnel of oaks you drove through earlier is also visible, a dark geometric line running for twenty miles in the sun gilded sea of pale grass.

*Notes*

Of course, as you'll probably note here, most people are so concerned over the problems they think await, they seldom see any beauty behind them.

The savanna now miles back, the road runs up and by a rare promontory housing twenty gnarled oaks and a wide yellow sign with Deer Crossing printed upon it in bold black letters. The oaks in various degrees of decay for fifty or more years somehow continue to stand, each trunk with a stitching of small punctures where swamp woodpeckers, self-appointed tree surgeons, try in vain to hasten the demise of these magnificent though far-in-decay oaks. Closer to the road, and you must slow to read this one, is a soiled wooden marker: Bethany Cemetery, Established 1780. Ten feet beyond, just before the scanty slate tombstones begin, is another sign, but this one is red and indicates the danger involved if we attempt to walk over the ancient corpses and rotted coffins. Not too many visitors stop here, but you of course are welcome if you so desire. However, it is getting late and it might be better to move along.

A few miles on well-manicured farms grace the roadside and on the right a huge white billboard with green scripted lettering reads: Dodd County. The sun has gone and a purple dusk floats in, but the driving is pleasant without a glare and even a novice would note the financial potential of the dark dirt farmland, but the scenery changes.

Cypress trees now push in on the road and strands of gray Spanish moss hang within inches of the top of your automobile. It's late in the day now as the sun went down much faster than anticipated. Chilled night air settles onto the stagnant dark water ditches along the road and a thin mist rises and swirls among the pine, oak and cypress trees.

You realize the temperature is not all that low, but still it's difficult to resist the urge to turn on the car's heater, and that's usually when most look up and see another sign. It's bent and riddled with small rusted holes, apparently someone has been using it for a little nocturnal scattergun practice. After all, all the locals know it's very important to have the right pattern, depending, of course, on what they plan to shoot. And this sign isn't held up by a post. No, see, it's nailed directly onto the tree. In fact, a portion of the bark has actually grown over an edge of the lettering. But it is still readable.

### Dodd County, Georgia

Largo, Ithaca, Moccasin Wallow
Known population—6600
Welcome to the Okefenokee

# – Excerpt –
# THE BEST
# DEER HUNTER
# IN DODD COUNTY

*Notes*

# EXCERPT
# (THE BEST DEER HUNTER IN DODD COUNTY)

He got dizzy and his mouth went dry and he shook violently, as much as the time he tried going cold turkey eight years back when his wife and kids walked out on Christmas day. Carp's head was spinning as everything went fast forward.

Screaming, he reached to shove the truck into reverse. But he was late. A pasty pale oval with glaring red eyes peered in from the shotgun side. Sandor held the flashlight beneath his face to spotlight a triumphant smile. With the other hand he dug his thumb behind his right eye, jerked the hand up and to the side, and with a wet sucking sound the eyeball popped out. The vacant socket filled quickly with a boiling gray thick mucus emitting vile-smelling wisps of smoke, while the eye, now in Sandor's hand, glowed and pulsed brighter with every beat.

Back against the door on the driver's side, Carp struggled to find the handle as Sandor reached through the glass, leaned close and held his throbbing eyeball near Carp's face. The best deer hunter in Dodd County sobbed, a choking sound, eyes rolling far back into his head. Sandor reached a little farther in and pinched Carp's eyelids and when he got the right grip, ripped them away—one by one. Now Carp was like a zombie, dead and alive, and nothing moved but his eyes and they'd been awakened to dart wildly with every dramatic move of his conqueror, his master.

"Not too bad a show, old Heath. You performed your role well. Of course not, of course you don't understand. Ridiculous of me. Why would I expect you to understand? Absolutely no competition left in this world."

Sandor walked away from the truck and freed his hands by sticking the eye into his mouth, held it there like a red grape, then worked a cartridge into the chamber of the thirty-thirty rifle. Carp's eyes quivered like those of a panicked deer caught in the headlights.

Now Sandor threw his head back, a wolf about to howl, and spit. The pulsating eye shot upward and flew fast toward the full moon. Then he aimed carefully, expertly made a fist around the stock and trigger, and

*Notes*

squeezed. The high sailing eye exploded into a million brilliant neon particles producing a glittering fireworks extravaganza before drifting still aglow back to earth.

Closer to the ground the fragments swirled together to reform the eye, now becoming a diamond-like brightness streaking at Sandor who merely reached up and caught it and stuck it back into his face as every animal in the Okefenokee began to howl, wail or scream a plaintive cacophony of protest from all God's creatures.

Sandor only laughed and, using the rifle as a baton, pretended to conduct the wild, wild hellish symphony. At the conclusion, when the swamp was quiet again, as the sun began to rise, Sandor turned and bowed magnificently as Carpenter Heath gasped his final breath.

# OUR FAVORITE TEACHER
## – Miss Power –

*Notes*

# EXCERPT (UNPUBLISHED POETS)

Miss Power's husband had been dead for well over twenty years. I guess that's why we called her Miss instead of Mrs., but come to think about it, in Ithaca we called every woman over fifteen Miss whether they were married or not.

Miss Power had seldom traveled far from Dodd County, except for her college days at Agnes Scott in Atlanta, but she was far more voguish than most Ithacans and the focal point of almost all educational and/or artistic endeavors in or near our town. Her daily style of dress was more emulative than imitative of Arquetta's daily style, and where most people weren't always convinced Cappy, Arquetta, Reverend Thomasson, or even Mr. Slim Benton had read every word of every book they said they'd read, you never doubted Miss Power if she held you with her intense gray-eyes stare and told you she'd just finished *This Side of Paradise*, *As I Lay Dying*, or even *War and Peace*. She was every bit as cosmopolitan as Arquetta and although no one dared come right out and say it, just as refined.

People who sat around and analyzed such social situations, and there were many in Ithaca and all across the south I'm sure, analyzed that since Miss Power's family tree admittedly could never match Arquetta Thorpe's family tree rooted in New England, Miss Power had palpably reinvented herself following Mr. Power's death when she'd gone off the deep end for a while and announced to the shock and despair of the community she'd decided to become a movie star like Greta Garbo. After the initial shock waves, most Ithacans, even some women, admitted looks would not be a problem. Miss Power's near stunning, petite figure, curly black hair and doe-like eyes had been well noted long before Mr. Power's heart gave out on him about thirty minutes after he and Mrs. Power kissed at midnight on New Year's eve when the tremendous siren went off atop The Farmacy (a quaint creation of a name by Phil Farmer for his pharmacy) as it did on all other special occasions like the end of a war, a tornado sighting, or if a fire broke out anywhere within the city limits.

Being discovered by movie people would be a huge challenge, especially

*Notes*

since Miss Power planned to retain her teaching position. Her personally architectured training program for movie stardom consisted of correspondence courses from New York and Los Angeles and several roles in productions with The Largo Players, a not-as-bad-as-we'd-thought-they'd-be theatrical group financially supported and led by Mary Smythe-Davison, a reluctantly aging, long-ago debutante from Savannah who'd purportedly studied drama at the University of Georgia, and while there met and married Darien Davison of Columbus, Georgia. As an attorney, Darien Davison would never amount to much, but financially, this was well reversed. Darien was the only child of the Davison's of Davison Tractor Manufacturers, reputed to have the inside track in Washington for most of the road building machinery to eventually be used in the construction of the nation's Interstate Highway system. The absence of success as a barrister gave Darien plenty of time to pursue his real love, other than Mary Smythe-Davison of course, quail hunting, and would eventually lead to the purchase of Pine Hills Plantation. This plantation of five thousand acres south of Largo, Georgia, was a turn-key, quail-hunting paradise replete with a private airstrip for VIP landings. It was never unusual to hear that a congressman or two were hunting out at Pine Hills and more likely than not a few months later we'd read or hear that Davison Tractor Manufacturers had signed a new government contract.

Since Darien's bride, Marianne, everyone called her Mary, Smythe came from "old money" in Savannah, one reporter cutely (long before reporters got cute) called the marriage a merger. Mary and Darien had quickly dropped from the academic rolls of Georgia to take a lengthy around-the-world honeymoon jaunt. In deference to Mary's theatrical yearnings, they spent the greater part of the trip in England where, Mary would later claim during the frequent high level cocktail parties held at Pine Hills, she'd studied theatre with attention to the Bard's works done at The Globe.

When asked, "Weren't all his works done at The Globe?"

The raven-haired Mary replied, "Perhaps, I'm an actress, not an historian. And you?" And in time and money, Mary became always the lead, and The Largo Players played always to packed houses (there was no admission) and always received grand reviews in the *Dodd County Democrat*, a weekly newspaper owned by Darien Davison.

Once Miss Power invited Arquetta and Cappy for a performance of Romeo and Juliet "and too for the reception" at Pine Hills following the performance. Later Miss Power admitted that long after she'd sensed she would never make it to Hollywood, she continued her performances with The Largo Players if for no other reason than the lavish post play receptions and other

*Notes*

fine parties at the plantation. When asked, by some of the perhaps jealous women of Ithaca, how she managed to resist any amorous advances by womanizing dignitaries frequenting these occasions, Miss Power would invariably raise her perfect eyebrows and say, "Did you hear that I did?"

# NIGHT QUESTIONS

*Notes*

# NIGHT QUESTIONS

The gurgling, sucking sound of the aspirator was getting to me. He'd been correct three days earlier when he'd lamented my impatience. Then his words had been clearer. Now he could barely communicate. Lou Gehrig's Disease does that, attempts to take all dignity as it takes all life, but the brain does go last, perhaps never with this victim, I thought as I stared down at the shriveled man before me. His mind showed no signs of surrender.

Beneath the aspirator's grinding sound, another noise more subtle, almost a buzzing, was constantly with us during the nights at the small old hospital. The lighting system, air conditioner, who would ever know? These noises are disturbing in the long quiet evenings, then indistinguishable during the days. My thought patterns matched the noises. Days, we could shake them, change them, but when night fell, when there was stillness, those tormenting thoughts of why, why him or why not me, returned. They test all we've ever known, those questions, those night questions.

Around three that morning I waked to his moan. "How long had he tried to get my attention?" I cursed myself for having fallen to sleep. He tried to smile and barely whispered. "You're just human." That's how it was with him. I could reveal my most denigrating truths but rarely feel judged or shamed.

As muscle strength attenuated, mental capacities soared. Such power from such weakness, and near the end, I imagined he read my mind and was getting into my mind as I struggled against thought of a man-made end to the suffering. But no, because you realize how precious the moments can be, each breath, each faint pulse.

Now he wanted me to talk of better times, old games, old happiness. I tried until the noise in the corridor let us know it was almost dawn. I spoke of the many games on the red clay field behind the school in Edison and recalled his once incredibly smooth songs. A faint smile from him here, wondering. For we'd all wanted him to chase fame, pursue his grand talent, but he'd chosen to stay home and hold it together for the family and, yes, friends. Certain towns need certain people. And I talked of all the things I'd learned from him—things we need when we play those bigger games in

*Notes*

larger stadiums, things we remember and hear instead of the crowd.

We, as always, saved the most cherished thoughts, memories of the hunt. Crisp winter dusk, when we blew upon our hands to warm trigger fingers as dogs trailed low before the point, our laughter at missed shots, maybe a congratulatory pat on the back. Then the intensity of the hunt would fade into an ensuing time of gratitude and appreciation before the fire as we thawed, drank, ate, and enjoyed our favorite conversations. He listened wearing that fixed grimace, somewhere between his great smile of old and a new mask involuntarily worn by those who face certain death. And just before they hustled in to bathe and rearrange things for another torturous day, a calm countenance flooded him and he whispered, "It will all be perfect." Then he winked, his wink which said so many words for so many.

And at that moment I didn't see the sunken eyes, the parched lips, or the concentration-camp body, and I no longer heard the horrible gurgling. For I saw him as he'd been and now would always be and I felt a Spirit answer all questions. Good bye dear friend. You changed it all for so many.

# – Excerpt –
# (UNPUBLISHED POETS)

*Notes*

# EXCERPT (UNPUBLISHED POETS)

Arm in arm they crossed Forty Seventh Street in the light snow. That night the snow was tinted red, sometimes greenish-blue falling against the glow of Christmas lights lining the sidewalks, lights vying for attention with the glaring neons of the small specialty shops so famous and close to Broadway. The three young people, a woman and two men, had their eyes on the Algonquin Hotel and maybe a nightcap while listening to Contessa play the blues. No holiday standards in The Blue Bar. Sometimes there they might get a glimpse of Faulkner in town to sign his latest contract, or maybe Hemingway tucked in a far corner as if daring a tourist to come near, yet with enough pale light on his face to be noticed by café society. Once the woman had talked briefly with Max Perkins, the only editor to understand modern writers, modern great writers. Nobody ever said they understood Max. Some might say he drank too much, while others in the same room might say they'd never seen him have more than two. And what about family? If he had one, they must have missed him. He was always in the city, out and about near Broadway, once in a while with a showgirl type, an older diva making a comeback. He'd also been seen with younger actresses, dancers and singers every now and then, but he loved the writers, the fiction writers, liked to help them with their manuscripts, help them celebrate their contracts with Scribners, liked to watch them bask in glory when books sold big, when they got a literary prize, especially then.

The young woman with two escorts wanted to write like that, fiction, but so far she'd not been so good. Not that this would matter or change her lifestyle, really. Her family had built great ships in New England for a hundred or more years and she was an only child. She'd self-published once and now lived in an elegant townhouse near Central Park where she had grand parties, but always after they'd dropped by the Algonquin. Someday she'd have the nerve to ask Maxwell Perkins, who might ask F. Scott Fitzgerald, or maybe even Hemingway. Anything was possible in The Blue Bar after midnight.

# JOE AND BRAIN

*Notes*

# EXCERPT (UNPUBLISHED POETS)
## JOE AND BRAIN

"Brain doesn't look all that happy, Skip." They watch the catcher as a pitch bounces off the edge of his mitt and rolls two or three feet away. Not bothering to get to his feet, he leans over, stretches his long arm and picks up the ball, giving it a close inspection before lobbing it back to the pitcher, Tuff Barnes, a reliever who spends more time practicing pitching than pitching, a chronic sore spot for the bullpen catcher, Moe Berg.

"Bergy's alright, probably just needs to cut back on the night life, little tired. Have you seen his latest? Makes you look twice. She's---------."

Tuff tosses the ball to Joe Cronin, the manager, and says, "Skip, that ball ain't scuffed none."

Cronin looks at the baseball and tosses it back to the pitcher. "Don't worry about it, Tuff. You want a new ball just get one." He points to the canvas ball bag with Boston Red Sox emblazoned on both sides. "You know how Moe is, if he drops one he wants everybody to think it had a scuff on it, some unusual movement or something."

"But that's just the thing, Skip, I thought that one did have some movement on it, 'cause that's my new pitch I been working on." He holds the ball nearer Cronin's face. "See, when I hold my thumb on the side like this—with this seam, it----------."

"Tuff, just get another damn ball and get on with it."

The pitcher, not known for out thinking the opposition (having once told a reporter he'd been traded to the Big F, Philadelphia) but blessed with a durable arm, gets back on the mound and glares down for a target, but now Moe is lying on his back using the mitt as a pillow and covering his mouth with a closed fist as if yawning. Tuff backs off the mound and says, "Guess Mr. Moe, does everybody know I went to Princeton, Berg can get away with anything 'round here. Guess maybe we got two sets ah rules 'round here."

Jack, the reporter standing nearby, blinks and says, "You hear that Skip?"

"Hear what I want to hear, see what I need to see, Jack. That's my secret." Now Joe Cronin holds his left hand up to eye level and uses the thumb of the

*Notes*

same hand to adjust the large silver ring. Some said he never removed the gaudy American League Championship ring, not even in the shower.

The reporter moves closer to the ring, inspecting it as if he hasn't inspected it at least twenty fives times since spring training. "Absolutely the greatest managing job ever in the game, Skip, I gotta admit, 1933, put the Yankees down by August. Damn."

"Could be, Jack. And Moe down there was a big part of it. Maybe you don't remember but in July he had to catch just about every game 'cause of injuries and we didn't miss a beat. In fact, we got hotter. But, then, McGraw's had some great years, too, but you know I ain't like him, Jack. I don't use a man up and then dump'em like he did Matty, but wait now, Jack, don't write that. We just talking like friends here. I-------"

"I know, Skip. You know I'm not like that, anyway. But I'll tell you right now. Lot of 'em are these days, the new ones are starting to change. They'll write anything anybody says, anytime, and some of 'em don't even wear ties on the beat. Especially in Cincinnati."

"Yeah, I know what you mean. You hear what that scumbag Tally wrote about me leaving the pitcher in to hit against Detroit last week? I couldn't believe he'd do me like that." Cronin stares at the ring again, adjusting it some with his thumb, looking at it like it's a crystal ball, a personal fortune teller.

"Well, you know you don't have to worry about me, Joe. You think I'd of lasted this long doing stuff like that?"

"Naw, naw, Jack. Everybody knows you're the best out there. I—-hey, Tuff. That one didn't move hardly at all."

"Huuhh, it didn't?" Tuff hadn't realized the manager still watched so closely.

"Tell you what, Tuff, you take this ball, not a scuffed place on it anywhere." Cronin rolls the new ball around in his hand, even lets the reporter see it. He figured this ingenious, letting the press feel like they were part of the club now and then. "Now show me and Jack here your new pitch."

The pitcher takes a deep breath, uses a big pump handle windup and fires the ball to the mitt, a perfect strike, perfect to hit, right down Broadway with absolutely zero movement.

Cronin yells down to Moe. "Hey, Bergy, what'd you think?"

From his knees, Moe lobs the ball back. But if you were alert, you'd notice he scrapes the ball on the ground during the movement of his arm back into throwing position. "Let me take another look, Joe, okay?"

Tuff catches the return throw and prepares to start another wind up. But Cronin steps directly in front of the mound. Aborting the wind up, Tuff stum-

*Notes*

bles and almost goes to the ground. The reporter holds the notepad in front of his face and Moe attempts to hide his amusement with his mitt. Tuff glares at them, but Cronin is talking again.

"Let me see that ball, Tuff."

With a puzzled expression, the rattled pitcher flips the ball to his manager. Without even looking at the ball, Joe tosses it to Jack.

"Well, I'll be——Hey, this ball is scuffed to hell."

"Not by me." Tuff says, almost like he's trying to convince himself.

"Take it easy, Tuff. Bergy did it, been doing it for years. A magician when it comes to doctoring the ball. Now get back up there and hold the rough place to your left with your two-seamer grip and motion to Bergy with your glove that you're gonna throw a fastball but it's gonna move in to a right-handed hitter."

Tuff stands atop the mound, eyes closed, mumbling, going over the instructions for the next pitch.

"And by the way, Tuff. That's why you need to show Bergy more respect. He can help you. Never been a man Bergy couldn't catch or help win. You probably don't even know he almost set a record for errorless games back in thirty, and—and here's something you might want to write down, Jack. And that's the secret of the whole game. See, a catcher can catch anything a pitcher's got, but he's gotta know what's coming, right? And on the other side of it, a hitter can hit just about any pitch if he knows what it's gonna be. But if he doesn't know, well, you know, even the good ones struggle to hit .300 and Cobb is the only one got to .400 much — but here's the kicker. Not too many want to admit it, but Cobb was pretty damn smart, almost smart as he was mean. Let's be honest here. Cobb could almost read a pitcher's mind. By that, I mean, he studied the game more than other players, particularly pitch sequences, patterns, and the pitcher's mannerisms, so close that at least seventy or eighty percent of the time he knew whether he was getting a fast one or a curve." Cronin stopped to get his breath. "Got all that, Jack?"

The reporter nods, looking at the notes as if someone has just handed him the original draft of The Declaration of Independence.

Tuff has a blank stare and says, "Want me to throw now, Skip?"

The reporter and Cronin laugh and the manager says, "Yeah, go ahead, son. Show me what you got." But when they turn to the plate, Moe's leaning against the corner of the stands near the bullpen, mask off, and a big grin on his face, talking to a woman wearing a white sun dress, huge Hollywood dark glasses and a wide brimmed straw hat to cover her pale face.

*Notes*

Cronin smiles. "Now would you look at this. The only guy in the game can attract as many women as——hey, Bergy. Would it be out of the way for me to ask you and the pretty young lady to give us a moment of your time so we can get this over with?"

The woman reaches over and pats the top of Moe Berg's sweat-stained turned-backward cap, and says, "Moe, do you ever feel overqualified for baseball?"

"Moe fakes a serious, faraway stare and then quickly shifts back to the flippant, devil-may-care persona he's perfected over the years. "Yeah, but the hours are great and I get more respect than if I'd practiced law." Soon he gets back into the catcher's stance, winces some as one of his knees pops and grinds.

Joe Cronin stares toward the plate, hands on his knees in a crouched position, a big cat, stalking prey. Jack is mesmerized, scribbling notes. Tuff takes a deep breath, and fires the ball home. The pitch flies to the mitt, darting wildly at the end.

Cronin, a very pleased look on his face, says. "Great, Tuff! Now you got it."

Jack whistles his admiration.

Moe gives the aviator thumbs up sign as he pulls off his mask and quickly turns his attention back to the young lady—not by herself now, as more and more fans crowd into Fenway for the afternoon game.

"But, Skip. That didn't have no pop in the mitt. I like to hear it pop!"

"That's why you got the highest-earned run average on the team, son. You've been pitching for the crowd—not to win. Anyway, that's Moe Berg down there catching. Softest hands in the business, lets the ball come to him. He could have made ol' Christy's fastball sound like it was landing in a pillow———now listen, go on and give me fifteen wind sprints, foul pole to foul pole."

Tuff gasps as he looks across the field. "Fifteen!!!! Fifteen??? Okay, Fifteen."

"Yeah, fifteen. That's how many years Moe's got in the big leagues, don't ever show up your catcher son."

Tuff flips his glove onto the bullpen bench and jogs off into the outfield. As they watch him run, Cronin says. "Hey, Jack. Ever wonder why they call it the foul pole instead of the fair pole?"

The reporter looks at the manager as if he's asked him how to make an atomic bomb. "No, but come to think about ----------."

Cronin interrupts, obviously pleased with himself. "Because if you think

*Notes*

about it, when a hitter hits the ball down the line and it hits the foul pole they call it a fair ball, right? Same way with the foul line."

"Damn, Joe. That's great stuff. When'd you come up with that?"

Cronin smiles his—nothing to it, really—smile and the two stand there silently for a while, occasionally glancing at Moe and the lady, the arrival of Boston's faithful fans and Tuff as he struggles to finish the fifteen sprints. The two men are comfortable with their silence, the crowd only a susurrus murmuring they'd tuned out long ago, never knowing what it meant to them.

Finally, Joe Cronin says. "You know, Jack. Sometimes the fans seem to be getting farther and farther away." Now he has a glassy stare as if he's a prophet waiting for a vision.

"Well, somebody better tell Brain."

Moe Berg and the young woman have moved onto the bullpen bench, holding hands and gazing at each other and definitely not discussing baseball.

One of the nearby fans puts a flask back into the inside pocket of his suit, points at Moe and the woman and yells at Cronin. "Hey, what kind of manger are you? Letting your players get away with that. No wonder we been losing lately."

A female fan rises from the next row, walks over to the heckler and clouts him across his boater with her sunbrella. Women loved Cronin. They thought he had that all-American look, that fair handsome look, as handsome as a movie star, but sunny, not the stormy, sexy Italian countenance that made women faint when they saw Valentino.

Joe Cronin laughs and takes his cap off and waves to the fans gathering close to the excitement, then yells to the culprit, "Hey, buddy, better go home and check on your wife. One of my starting pitchers didn't show up today." Each section cheers loudly as they recognize the manager and nearer the dugout someone asks, "Hey, Joe! You gonna let Brain play today?"

"Naw, not today. Ain't you heard—we're trying to win." He left them laughing and applauding as he ducked into the dugout. But he was trying not to think about the end, the last time he'd leave the field. There couldn't be much after that.

# THE DRAGON SLAYER

*Notes*

# EXCERPT (UNPUBLISHED POETS)

"The bright yellow Spad flew fast toward the observation balloon, a hulking mass of hydrogen filled canvas looming like a dirty tan tear shaped cloud in the pale first light. Aimed at the slit in the network of two-inch cable holding the five balloons in formidable formation above the startled German gunners scrambling to their positions within the dense ground fog that has ghostly formed a second smooth gray surface for the charred battle-rugged earth, the biplane turns sideways and dips crazily, then miraculously smoothes out just before it shoots through the gap in the wire and begins to climb fast, the one-hundred horsepower Mercedes engine clattering a harsh warning against the pressure and heat of the sudden acceleration. The gunners below, unable to get off even one round, stare mesmerized as if watching a film of the moment they've dreaded since word of this wild man, this Dragon Slayer, reached the trenches. They know what's coming, too, and begin to run from their positions, some still craning their necks, unable to take their eyes from the spectacular but deadly attack. Now the plane is upside down flying back over the top and they see the pilot hold several sticks of dynamite to his smoking cigar, the sticks held together by a blue scarf. The fuse sparkles brilliantly in the low light as the dynamite topples toward the very top of the center of the balloon and now it's a race for the pilot to climb away hard from the exploding monster he's created."

Cappy pauses, lets me catch up. I flex my writing hand and take a deep breath, realizing I've held it since the beginning of the narration, the entire last, long paragraph. It doesn't matter, I have a few minutes to relax now as he stares into the fire. Once again there is no doubt my grandfather is one of the great raconteurs. And why not? He'd lived the stories, not merely made them up like most of the old men who sat around in front of Mr. Slim Benton's two-pump Gulf gas station and grocery store telling tall tales. Except for Snakeman, of course, his stories were true and accurate, especially in clear weather, and most of them had already been recorded in Mr. Slim's daughter's newspaper in the weekly historical section. But if the day got dark nobody listened to Snakeman, because in bad weather he'd even

*Notes*

curse and say just about anything, which we thought was probably excusable. He was at least ninety five years old, probably nearer a hundred, and the only one from Dodd County still around from the Civil War. This made Snakeman a sort of celebrity even after the historical section of the paper recorded he'd been a drummer boy—and had not ridden with cavalry defending Savannah. That didn't alter the fact he only had one arm, although Mr. Loring and at times Mr. Slim (depending on the audience) said Sankeman had lost the limb to a Massey Ferguson corn puller and not to a Union saber.

At one point in time in Snakeman's seemingly eternal life, Dr. Slattery was asked, by whom specifically we many never know, to examine that stump of an arm to determine which story we should believe. A rather difficult task considering Snakeman's age, not to mention the doctor's training or lack of training for the peculiar assignment. As usual, Cappy took a different slant when asked what he thought about the strange suggestion being put to Dr. Slattery. "I'm not surprised by the request." Here his bemused gaze swept the, all eyes on the boards, checker players, except for Mr. Slim now looking to heaven as if wondering why they allowed Cappy Thorpe to ever gain the floor. "What surprises me is that our good doctor would waste time honoring it."

"Maybe he just wants to know the truth," Mr. Loring said.

"Don't think Mr. Cappy ever worries 'bout the truth." Mr. Stanley, town atheist, said.

"Now boys, y'all know you ought not talk like that about a man who actually had a glass of wine with the Red Baron." Mr. Slim said. It took about thirty seconds for the laughter to fade, but as it did the men looked up from the boards, waiting, knowing Cappy couldn't back away from this one.

Cappy didn't smile. He would joke around with the best of them from time to time, but not about the Great War, or more specifically, his participation in the Great War. And I noticed that Mr. Hyde look I dreaded so much darken my grandfather's face as he said, after looking at and polishing with his coat cuff the too large, especially for the day-to-day life in Ithaca, and especially for his bony fingers, Harvard ring, "No, I'm sure you don't believe or understand that story. This would be difficult for you after spending the war watching black men pick cotton."

I closed my eyes as he finished, readied myself for maybe a flying walking cane or coke bottle or even checkerboard. But there was only a loud silence, if you follow me, until Mr. Slim said, "Stop mumbling, Cappy, we couldn't make out a word you said."

Long known as a master of the dramatic theatre-like exit, my grandfather

*Notes*

was already briskly walking away speaking to himself in Latin as the checker players began to laugh and talk and enjoy their games as if nothing had happened, and of course nothing really had happened if the men had not heard what Cappy said. If. I rolled the little big word around in my head, not realizing I'd locked a dead straight stare on Mr. Slim, until he said, for my ears only. "You'll figure it out someday, boy. If you don't end up trying too hard to do it."

"Yessir." What else can you say when you're thirteen?

Mr. Slim continued. "And whether you believe it or not, we all may not act like we like that ol'Dragon Slayer," (Cappy had told everybody in town, at least twice, the nickname given him by the Germans after he'd developed the unique upside down dynamite bombing method used against the observation balloons) "but most of us hold a lot of respect for him—even if what he says probably ain't exactly all—well you know." As he'd talked he'd pointed to my grandfather ambling along, now across the railroad tracks on to the center of town and his law office. There, he'd probably "have a small taste of beverage" while planning his next sortie against the relentless crew of semi-enemy gunners disguised as retirees playing checkers.

I looked at Mr. Slim Benton without really looking at him and said, "Yessir," again. Then I followed Cappy into town. There didn't seem to be much else to do at that moment and anything was better than being left between the trenches in "no man's land."

# WHERE DREAMS END

*Notes*

## EXCERPT (LEGENDS, DEMONS AND DREAMS)
## WHERE DREAMS END

When he sat at the bar he thought of a comeback, as all drunks must think to survive. When he walked back to the apartment in the dusk of Tybee Island, he thought of the little girl in Ithaca struggling for identity in the aftermath of the divorce. When he drank again, late, on the porch facing the shipping channel into Savannah, he cried. For there would be no return.

Days passed each the same, until there came a time when he was not the man who had played so long in the NFL, a time when the large, handsome Super Bowl ring sat pompously yet sadly within the dusty-glassed cabinet of the Abercorn Pawn Shop.

Tybee absorbed all, and he continued to make the walk to the Driftwood, vowing to quit drinking, go back, make amends, maybe coach, knowing he was still great with fundamentals. But each evening he returned along the golden marshes until there came a day when he looked like the others, only a scintilla remaining of the athlete, the past, fading, almost gone, almost as if never there.

Then one January morning only minutes before dawn, and of course on Sunday, the flashing red lights of an ambulance bounced against the gray, weather worn apartments and over the thin layer of loitering ghost-like marsh fog. The young driver switched on the siren as they roared back to Savannah, knowing the ride was far too long for this one. He'd seen it many times. Out here they died at dawn.

Some had been famous, like this one, now forgotten, ignored, as the island took them in, made them one, then spit them out and raced them too late for Savannah.

Later along the coast, another pristine morning, and some fine people stroll the strand of dark sand while others breakfast calmly upon a condo veranda and view the Atlantic. Still, someone opens a bar, perhaps the Driftwood, and a customer or two faithfully arrive. No choice, really, even knowing where that first drink will take them.

Tybee Island, last stop on the edge of Georgia, on the edge of sanity, where dreams end.

# AN AFFINITY OF
# OLD HUNTERS

*Notes*

# ITHACA, GEORGIA
## 19??

I am very old and I have seen many panthers. I've killed three. A more relentless man, my grandfather totaled eight. Their heads hang there above the fireplace. Tomorrow I go for another.

The government people claim there are only a thousand or so down in the Everglades. I disagree. We have that many even here in the Okefenokee.

People call them cougars, pumas, catamounts, panthers. I am amused. They are all the same for me, wildcats with long J-shaped tails and very sharp teeth. I've been after them for years.

The agencies are incorrect with their estimates, but if you share my experiences with government people, you realize this isn't exactly unusual.

But now I've claimed three. Their heads stare down, their glassy eyes reflect the flame, their hides warm rugs upon the hearth. And tomorrow will be cold, near twenty by dawn when I plan to leave this fire. That's when he'll move. Yes, he's wary, he senses my stalk.

I have just finished cleaning the .12 gauge double barrel. This will be a very close kill. There is a calculated chance he'll jump me near the lair, like the third one so many years ago. This happens if a stalk is protracted and things get turned around. So the double barrel is best for tomorrow. An automatic might jam, a pump could hang, or, I might miss a moving shot with a rifle, and there are no second chances when they leap.

This cat is a good one, just the sort to turn the tables and hunt the hunter. An inexperienced hunter would be in a great amount of trouble with this one. You see, luck is not a factor when you set out to kill a panther. And when, not if, a novice failed, he could never expect to return and get that particular cat. They never forget a hunter

An older hunter is another matter. In time you will learn there is strength in age as surely as there is strength in youth, just in another form. At a certain age a hunter doesn't worry about wounds or even death. But true, where a younger man fears actual death an older hunter harbors more curiosity about the unknown that follows death. My grandfather never revealed his

*Notes*

theories about this unknown. While young and old alike pray E. M. Forster was far from the mark as he wrote. "Our final experience, like our first, is conjectural. We move between two great darknesses." I must ask him about this near midnight as we confer when we share a spirit or two. He'll be here. Strange how close we've become through the years, much closer than when he was alive. I'm certainly not as lonely as I was out here with him when I was a boy. Regardless, at night when I keep a fire, he returns. For a while he's silent, until after we drink. I'll add some wood now because his time is near.

I've almost alienated myself from the folks of Ithaca (or is it the other way around). For even today they persist in questioning my grandfather's sanity, and to be candid, knowing the agrarians as I've come to, they probably insinuate the same of me.

Now I must rest. The shot tomorrow will be a close one, maybe less than fifteen feet, and only those who hunt, and true, those who have been hunted, understand such a kill.

# CENTER STAGE

*Notes*

# CENTER STAGE
## EXCERPT (LEGENDS, DEMONS AND DREAMS)

Late in the season-----------

He didn't think of himself as old. The years disagreed and the years never lie, just pass and pass to experience, a subtle relentless accumulation, like a three-two count. Now everything rides on one pitch.

So only the old man is left, a battle field promotion, the others fallen to umpires. There are those games when the opposition gets all the calls, appears destined to win, but winning is never a gift and the game stays close, low scoring, and the enemy squanders chances, their leaders unable to handle charity, and as the day wears on fate bows to ability.

He sits in the bullpen and studies every play, every pitch, yet sometimes drifting back to lost chances and personal setbacks, career catastrophes of heavy drinking, night life, even racism, even reverse discrimination, part of the game in those days. Now he hangs for a pension, so he can stumble homeward to the small town and maybe rest, maybe not. There are bills and bills from decades of minor league pay.

He's being signaled to center stage after all the years, all the innings. Now they ask him to manage in the big leagues, the supreme, elusive dream, once a certainty when he was the bright star, heir apparent to a baseball throne to lead the team to a championship. He ambles past the packed house. A few pure fans show recognition and shout encouragement. Others laugh and some younger ones not understanding the game pelt him with beer cups and obscenities. They fear the game in his hands.

But he's different now. This is not the same quiet senior figure the players see each day in the clubhouse. He's still wrinkled beyond repair, skin like darkened leather, teeth dull from age, tobacco and coffee, and there are a few stains on the front of the white uniform. But the shoulders are rolling up and the eyes are different, maybe transformed back forty years when he was a presence, when he'd fight savagely even a hint of dissension or insubordination. Anxious to help, the entire infield gathers at the mound. Pennants are often won by a single game. Champions understand this and

*Notes*

play as if each game will be the most important one of the season. Cellar dwellers think they have time, time to get it going, no sense of urgency. They view the season as a grind, not a privilege.

Champions live the moment, champions always, each day, each pitch. So the shortstop says. "Jam, Tano, he likes it soft away." And the third baseman blurts. "Yeah, give 'em the gas, he wants the curve."

The old man nods, but says, "We'll put Tano on. Next hitter, Wilson, is good alright, but he's right handed and doesn't have much power."

Someday the shortstop will manage the team, maybe only five years or so down the road. "Hey, no way. Tano's got twenty bags and Wilson's been hitting .300 all year."

The coach grimaces, loves the shortstop, admires him, knows he'll be a solid manager, but says flatly, "Then we'll pitch out—three times." The others smile and withdraw, having gone as far as they want to go.

The shortstop glares, some hard words rising inside, but he's got too much class and reaches with his glove and punches the old coach lightly on the arm, then retreats to his position. Baseball has its ways and he honors the built in respect. Someday it will be his.

He is a talented player and respects the game. He never takes steroids. He never needs a "greenie." He never turns a kid away for an autograph, and after every game he is a winner, regardless the score. He is a champion.

# THE HOUR
# BEFORE DUSK

*Notes*

# THE HOUR BEFORE DUSK

One man looked like Abraham Lincoln, the other hunter had a great smile. Both had coarse, creased, outdoor worker's skin. Life hadn't always been easy.

On the surface, Lincoln appeared stern, troubled, almost mean, but his past disagreed. The other, Smile, was an open book, trusting, naïve, as if tomorrow would take care of itself. He lived for the moment, one covey at a time. The stern one was often preoccupied, but he enjoyed a hunt—in his odd way.

Their obedient dogs zigzagged before them as they hunted a vast field of golden broom-sedge. They'd found many coveys away from the edge—where birds weren't supposed to be, easy targets. Following tradition, they shot only two birds from each point. They could have taken many, for now they were much better shooters, and tomorrow there would be just as many birds. But they'd never been greedy and some things never change.

Both hunters kept an eye on the cut in the pines. Yes, maybe today. They'd waited a long time for the next hunter. They watched the sun slide and the cold shadows grow, his time of day. He would arrive within the hour before dusk. He preferred to hunt then, when dogs revived, when quail moved best, when serenity inundated the land.

And the new hunter walked through the opening into the swaying sedge, looked at his hands, moved them tentatively and admired the newfound flexibility. Smile offered an ultra-light twenty gauge, a gun the new shooter had always needed for quail. Such a fine pattern the side-by-side double would have. He swung it, sighted, and nodded his approval.

They hunted until the pale magenta sky gradually turned black, and they allowed the new man to lead. He'd always had an almost mystical insight for birds—and not only for bird hunting, but for all life, too.

Content there with the sport, they felt so good, for it hadn't always been that way. Arm in arm they walked toward Ithaca, not weary as in the past. Along the way the new one sang, surprised at the recaptured beauty of his voice. The other two hummed harmony until they came upon the house.

*Notes*

Their home, really so small, but there had always been enough room, enough food, enough love.

There she waited, arms ready. She'd yearned for her youngest, never dreaming he'd be next. Smile and Lincoln watched her embrace their brother. They winked knowingly, for he'd always been her favorite. And God held them as they waited for the others.

# – Excerpt –
# UNPUBLISHED POETS
# 1935

*Notes*

# EXCERPT (UNPUBLISHED POETS)
## 1935

Baseball players say there is no way to prepare yourself. You always think it will be somebody else. So Amby Duncan hadn't seen it coming, especially not the day after the All Star game at Comiskey Park in Chicago, the Negro League East-West Classic, a gala three-day event far surpassing the Major League Classic held in Boston, at least in style and exuberance, and with much more flair, according to one major league owner wishing to remain anonymous.

Of course, Satchel Paige and Josh Gibson had stolen the show, and sartorially, as was always the case, Satch had stolen the show off the field as well, parading the Palmer Hotel lobby in his white linen suit, high-collared well-starched shirt and perfectly knotted, brilliant purple tie. It was said all Satchel Paige's clothes were imported, mostly from Italy, and he invariably purchased duplicate outfits, always causing a stir at dinner as other customers murmured and wondered how his attire remained so fresh through the day in the summer heat. Satch was a true entertainer and a genius at promoting himself as well as the game of baseball.

When asked by a younger reporter about the black and white shoes, Satchel crossed his long legs bringing one of the shoes into more prominent view for all in the hotel lobby and said as if he'd just thought of it, "My two toners remind me of our two big leagues all right here in one country, playing right in the same ball-parks but never with or even against each other. A real shame, too, but you know what, bad as things are like that, I predict that someday, maybe even a whole lot sooner than some folks want to think about, there's gonna be just one major league—all of us playing together."

The young reporter wrote furiously, catching up while Satch caught his breath and nodded to mingling fans and continued to sign autographs, often taking the time to write "Don't look back, somebody might be gaining" on a ball now and then, particularly for some of the better looking ladies. This always amused several other players there in the lobby, smiling and talking mostly to each other, probably feeling invisible in the world Satchel Paige

*Notes*

had created for himself.

Realizing he was on to more than a baseball story, the reporter asked, "So Satch." Satchel raised his eyebrows just a little. "I mean, Mr. Paige, say the leagues do go together, well then, I was wondering if you'd change the color of your shoes."

Under his breath, as he watched a lady, for whom he'd just autographed her blouse's cuff, walk back to her circle of friends, her ample hips swaying hypnotically, at least for him, Satch said. "College boy, huh."

"Sir?"

"I said, have you seen us play?"

"Yessir. Many times, I-----"

"Okay, so?" Satch spread his arms, palms up for an unspoken answer, palms becoming starkly pink beneath the brilliant Palmer House chandeliers.

"You'd wear all black shoes, wouldn't you Sa--, I mean, Mr. Paige?"

"And why would I do that, son?"

"Because when they let you play in the majors together, there won't ever be any more question. Who's best."

Satchel rose and said, "Tell you the truth, I'd probably wear gray and if you print it all just like we said it, you just might get a prize or something." Then Satchel Paige looked hard down at the reporter. "You will put this in the paper, won't you?"

"Of course I will Mr. Paige, this is great stuff, fantastic, I-----"

Satch nodded and walked away, the way he ended all interviews. Like he said, never look back. But he might have been thinking about the many times similar exchanges with the press had not been printed, got ambushed somewhere in higher places. Maybe this white writer was different. The younger ones seemed to be, but the older ones would never change and they were taking a long time to die. He signed the very last autograph and waved goodbye to the crowd, knowing the other players were glad to see him go, go change for dinner into a different but same outfit. He smiled at the thought, but also he was thinking about the bad luck that the Babe had retired in May. He'd always wanted to play against Ruth, always wanted to strike him out in Yankee Stadium. Satchel Paige was also thinking about Amby Duncan's bad luck, if you could call it that. He slammed his palm hard against the door of the elevator. But he made sure to use his left hand.

Ambrose, Amby, Duncan sat on the very last seat of the bus and stared at the countryside, going over a lifetime of memories. Some good, some bad, some he'd not thought of in years. Maybe this was good, this back-

*Notes*

ward thinking, get the future off his mind. The future was going back home to Ithaca, Georgia. Not all that bad under different circumstances, but not like this, released, and released in the locker room right in front of everybody immediately after the game, all the All-Stars looking dead at him along with the police and the owner of the team. Only Satch had come over and offered to try and help. But even he shied away when he heard who was behind it all, and now they knew it was the only safe solution. It was hard, but certain folks you didn't mess around with in Chicago. It was a hard way alright, but the only way Amby would ever leave town alive.

# THE GENIUS OF
# T.S. AND OSCAR

*Notes*

# THE GENIUS OF T.S. AND OSCAR

*"Poetry is an escape from personality."*
**T.S. Eliot**
Circa 1919


*"Literature anticipates life."*
**Oscar Wilde**
Circa 1881

# PYRRHIC
# VICTORY

*Notes*

# PYRRHIC VICTORY

It's like being trapped in one of those box canyons in a western movie, no way out except to fight. Now you have to play and you always claim you won't come back, when it's bad, when you're humiliated, bewildered, and they curse you at the bottom of the pile, but if you retaliate you're out of the game, just what they want, and anyway, don't let them know it gets to you, then it is worse. So play your way out, step by step, yard by yard, each at once a victory, but at what cost?

You're saying it's the last time, knowing deep it isn't because you'll forget like a drunk forgets the pain, drinks again for an inexplicable reason, not important anyway, for once the drink takes the man it never matters why.

Here it is the same, in the canyon where the pressures and shadows grow near the end, late, where you forget, return to have dignity and pride bashed, exploited by those born to maim the total man, but so you know that and still try again, play again, all we can know or risk after a certain point, the only way to be somebody when it's all we understand.

So try to gouge my eyes, and knee my groin and curse me close where only I can hear, but you can't make me quit. Not today! Just get through this game, this play really.

And so I run and run as if in a trance. But I won't drop that ball and I won't miss that signal, not now. For I'm in the game, and what I once thought defeat I now consider growth.

**AB**
Circa---late eighties

*"We still have to take that journey inside ourselves,*
*spiritually and psychologically."*
**Bill Moyers**

*Notes*

## MORNING MUSE

To sit quietly near the big window
To the early sun
Long cherished long mornings
Coffee in a clear cup
Trying to collect a rambling muse
Dappled dreams of might have been
Staring at the keys, an hour-glass, too
Bright sun splaying the pond
So it doesn't look cold out there
But the oak out front rattles
As the evergreens wave off a northeast wind
Stoke the low fire now and wonder aloud
Could she be thinking of me?

*Notes*

# SLATON'S SECRET

There is no magic fountain,
Cream, pill or trick injection,
No haunting chant from some far mountain,
Not even prayer halts time's infection.

If my friend you have a doubt,
Please face the hard truth mirror
That makes men cringe and ladies pout,
Brings stitch and scalpel nearer.

Yet there is an ebony lady
Who always looks and acts
As if she's rested where it's ever shady
To stay calm and face all life's attacks.

Can you guess her age,
Where is the expected wrinkle,
Or is she made up for the stage,
How can aged eyes so beguile and twinkle?

She claims no magic potion,
Has made no devilish deal
Nor sailed some distant ocean
To change a century's unmerciful will.

Complexion smooth and eyes so clear,
Hair silver, trimmed and fine,
Voice pure and mellow without any fear,
Where'd she get this tell us—we'll form a line!

*Notes*

Serious schemers miss the hour,
And yet not really proven we of course know
That beauty from within has special power
For those who feel not plan it so.

Please lady hold your kindness,
Wisdom and experience dear
And forgive those who were mindless,
Harmed you or caused you fear.

And did your saintly smile mask any rage
For perhaps a careless few
Who couldn't turn life's changing page?
My God, if they only knew.

*"True tolerance can never be conquered
and forever beware anyone who tries."*
**AB** circa 1939

*Notes*

## DISGUISED GORE

Finally I knew,
The serpent was evil, evil, evil
And fear burning my mind
As bones shake beneath a defeated stare
Of red lifeless eyes.

Closer to my lips, bottle seeking
A weary face of sunken lines
Withdrawn of hope, downcast dark
Before the stinking sweat
Of another lost day of many
Thousands gone, disappear.

Nearer the edge, peering past
A bottomless reflection
Of observer and observed
Dying a suicidal reckoning,
Life and death as well bowing
To waiting glasses of disguised gore.

Drifting out now, restless spirit rest
And wild rest the unholy fear of it there
Coiled close beneath my chin of vomit,
And if I think it there will end it, too late.
Praise fast something now, awake to die
Forever, at last.

*Notes*

# BODY COUNT

General Custer was an officer and a gentleman.
They say.
A dashing young hero lieutenant cavalry-man
And a great leader during The War Between The States,
Always out front of the charge,
Hair flowing blond, saber glistening
For God and glory against the south,
So easy to dehumanize then,
As the Sioux would later be
When he would free them
Of their freedom by murdering
Warriors—some not.
But then when thought invincible at last
He heard about the dream
Crazy Horse dreamt,
That he could not die in battle
And now both had never lost
And true warriors never say never
Until they meet and know.

They made certain they would clash
As the greatest warriors forever will.
So the Little Big Horn was born
An inevitable battle,
The civilized against the savage
But now even God could not know
The difference
And so they fight on
In Viet Nam.
In Iraq
In------------
In-------
In----

*Notes*

# FALL FIFTIES

After the harvest, teepees
They appear, nocturnal
Frost fallen
White

Stacks of peanuts olden
Blanket of moon
Late October
Night

Windless, clear, quiet
Faraway grave
Never be old
All's right

*Notes*

## SUMMER NIGHTS

Little Richard, Elvis and Fats,
Their songs blared into those nights,
Driving downtown, real cool cats,
Better by far than having gang fights.

After the drive-in show,
Listening to Nashville till one.
Where did those old times go?
Small town boys, small town fun.

*Notes*

# A TWIST

"Never let a selfish motive prevent an act of kindness."
**Alex Blackstone**
Circa – 1988

Originally this quote was attributed to my grandfather but segued to Alex Blackstone as he became my alter-ego upon my return from rehab (Charter by the Sea, St Simons Island, Georgia). Through the Grace of God and a one-day-at-a-time Alcoholics Anonymous program, I've not as yet returned. So if by chance someone you know has a drinking problem and desires help, it is as near as our knees. All we have to do is ask. He is always there at the door, knocking, waiting for us to come to our senses—and ask Him for Grace. And no matter our circumstances, or what we've been through, or put our loved ones through, the door will miraculously fall open and a remarkable, yes miraculous, solution will appear. I can only tell you what happened to me. There is no power greater than God's Love, Forgiving Spirit and Unconditional Grace. Imagine, free of charge, perfect freedom.

Now, my friend, let's have another cup of coffee and thanks for listening. We may well have just experienced an AA meeting, where, by the way, the only requirement for attendance is a desire to stop drinking.

*Notes*

# AN AREA OF GRAY

Sadly enough for southerners
The Civil War had to be fought
To end slavery.

Sadly enough for northerners
The Civil War was not fought
To end racism.

Sadly enough for all Americans
We did not first honor
The Emancipation Proclamation.

*Notes*

# DUSK DEPENDABLE

They don't change with fortune's change,
Each day staying true,
As steady as the relentless sun,
As persistent as the winter rain,
Revealing as a moon at full
To pale our darkest hour,
Unequivocally, unconditionally reliable,
Exactly as we first knew them
Waiting still at the end of all days,
Comforting, scintillating, inspiring,
As sunsets,
Brilliance upon brilliance of God's genius
Waiting still at the end of all days,
Old books, our old books, our old friends.

*Notes*

## MINERVA SLEEPS

Few writers can
Resist a clean blank page.
But there are many clean blank pages
Resisting writers.

*Notes*

# DREAM PASSAGE TWELVE

The town's good doctor sent
His trusted right-hand man
Who drove us with a determined glint
To dark eyes knowing well the plan.

Out near Cordray's in a moon-paled field,
Torch flames leapt to the sky.
Six of us were to complete the deal,
Only two knew exactly why.

We all hunkered down near the fire
And there in the November night's chill
Watched the doctor aim and fire an aught six
Into a grand old buck for the kill.

Then the black man revealed a long knife
To sever the artery carotid
And drained the blood, red as all life,
As our hearts and stomachs all knotted.

Eight eyes bulged when we saw the slide
Of the red stuff into the cup
Which had inscribed on its silver side,
"You'll soon be a man—drink up."

Jimmy the son was naturally first,
I was amazed at his aplomb.
He took a swallow as though there were thirst,
Then handed friend Sammy some.

Black-haired Sammy trembled more than a little
Yet courageously held out his hand,
Jimmy complied with a grin of red spittle,
Sammy winced, took a sip, was a man.

*Notes*

Next they looked not at me but to Dennis,
Standing more than a bit from the fire,
But always one there for the finish,
He held up the cup as I swore my eyes liar.

Then five of them turned to leer,
All surely men by now
And as I accepted with considerable fear
Some demons from hell began to howl.

With that unearthly wail I awoke
And screamed my dream's fear to the night
Until grandmother appeared and began to soak
Away sweat from the nightmare's fright.

So beware tales told to a child
Of rituals on the passage to man.
For they will probably rest dormant all the long while
Or—some night get far out of hand.

*Notes*

# PAST IMPERFECT

Charlie Tea could throw it ninety five and don't ignore the book that said his curve seemed to come alive as it exploded into a vicious hook. Once we watched him hurl a game against Morgan, an admirable foe, but their hitters swung like they were tame as Charlie cut down twenty like grass beneath the mow.

Did he ever pitch in the Series? Why wasn't he a pro? Who will answer such disturbing queries? Whose conscience does not hurt him so? See, Charlie was of a different time, when different people played on different fields, while nowadays we question why life was so unkind and some were dealt a hand which didn't match their skills.

But those neon bright and brilliant white lights surely pulled hard on boys like Charlie and me as we yearned to play in stadiums packed so full, and really, how could they have ever known, if they'd asked we'd have played for free. But the reality of our lives now raises its hard-knocked face and soon we admit, even to our wives, we're finally content at the old home place.

Because there's nothing quite as sad as those who live in yesteryear, and talk of times when they were yet a lad, to unknowingly reveal their maddening inherent fear. So, Charlie Tea, let's you and I and others not worry about what might have been, but try to treat all as brothers, do what fate puts before us and know God before the end.

Note: *Charlie Tea Duncan is a character from the novel* Unpublished Poets *and the son of Amby Duncan from Ithaca, Georgia. Amby Duncan caught and pitched for ten years for the Pittsburg Crawfords in the Negro Leagues during the nineteen thirties. Charlie Tea Duncan, a sidearm pitcher, won twelve straight games in 1945 for the Ithaca Black Senators, the only all black team (except for the catcher) to ever participate in the state finals of the Ty Cobb Sandlot League.*

*Notes*

# SALEM FAITH

Shock of it floods
Community so close,
January moans, February wails,
Winter dead.

Six carry to the cross and candles,
Prayer, then Salem,
Frozen earth
Gone.

After the dirt falls,
The sad smiles and nervous laughter
Until the young cry,
Puzzled.

Years on always drift away,
Only time passages
Teach so hard
So well.

No! Not final you dark shroud!
Light prevails, save those gone!
And those here be April reborn
To live anew again
Until fear dies first.

*Notes*

# CAPPY'S TRUE FREEDOM

The most striking, powerful, example of God's Grace
and Beauty—the Christian slave with more inner peace
than his Christian owner/master.

**Cappy Thorpe**
Harvard—Class of 1922

Carlton O. "Cappy" Thorpe is a character
from the novel *Unpublished Poets*.

*Notes*

# TIME FLIES

Click, tick and drip-------
Lake cabin far in the south----------
Wooden ceiling fan, old wind-up clock and a leaky faucet------
Where we live out life outside of life with only one friend------
Time flying fast with everything slowly slowing----------
Mind blending impatient stories with patient words--------
As the big window plays a silent movie outside-----
Also inside it's still, so quiet, except for the click, tick and drip----
And there seems to be time but you know you never know-------
So sometimes it comes and often it goes----------
Those words, those sentences, perhaps some poetic prose-------
Could come together and magically flow to a brilliant beginning---
That passes too fast to the long hard middle, that struggle within---
Or the relentless, inevitable, all-too-soon end----------
Of the click and the tick and the drip.

*Notes*

# WALK THE WALK

When I was younger than young
Before I counted years or tears
Or thought about an end
I bravely approached the ancient lawyer
With whom I lived.
Old I say, maybe he was fifty and five
When I asked for the family car,
There was not the slightest pause
Before the startling, "no."
And as to why
He said, "Your hair is way too long."
Grandmother, my refuge from all life's early trials,
Stood behind her mate of some thousand years
And pointed to a picture of our Savior.
So, I too pointed then stammered, "Well,
My hair's no longer than His."
Again not the slightest pause.
"True, and He did a heap of walking too.
Didn't He, boy?"

# NO
# PERSONAL
# PARDONS

*Notes*

# A SENTENCE FOR BILL CLINTON

"Therefore it is necessary for a man of the governing class to set about regulating his personal conduct and character."

**Confucius**
459 B.C.

# SHAKESPEARE'S
# BLOOM

*Notes*

# FIFTEEN NINETY NINE

For who not needs shall never lack a friend

**Hamlet**
From: *Hamlet*


Who steals my purse steals trash—'tis something-nothing,
"Twas mine, 'tis his, and has been slave to thousands-
But he that filches from me my good name
Robs me of that which not enriches him
And makes me poor indeed.

**Iago**
From: *Othello*


Let us once lose our oaths to find ourselves
Or else we lose ourselves to keep our oaths.

**Berowne**
From: *Love's Labour's Lost*


That one may smile, and smile, and be a villain.

**Hamlet**
From: *Hamlet*

*Notes*

# TRANSCENDENT

In Shakespeare, characters develop rather than unfold and they develop because they reconceived themselves. Sometimes this comes about because they overhear themselves talking, whether to themselves or others. Self overhearing is their royal road to individuation, and no other writer before or since Shakespeare, has accomplished so well the virtual miracle of creating utterly different yet self-consistent voices----------

**Harold Bloom**
Circa---1998

# HOW COULD HE HAVE KNOWN

We are lived by drives we cannot command, and we are read by works we cannot resist. We need to exert ourselves and read Shakespeare as strenuously as we can, while knowing his plays will read us more energetically still. They read us definitively.

**Harold Bloom**
Circa---1998

Glory is like a circle in the water,
Which never ceaseth to enlarge itself
Till by broad spreading it disperse to naught.

**Shakespeare's**
Joan of Arc

*Notes*

# ELIOT'S GREAT ENIGMA

*Notes*

# ELIOT'S GREAT ENIGMA

*Excerpt*: The Waste Land
By: **T.S. Eliot**

Who is the third who walks beside you?
When I count, there are only you and I together
But when I look ahead up the white road
There is always another one walking beside you
Gliding wrapped in a brown mantle, hooded
I do not know whether man or woman
------ But who is that on the other side of you.

# SAMUEL TAYLOR COLERIDGE

*Notes*

From: *The Rime Of The Ancient Mariner*
By: **Samuel Taylor Coleridge**

The self-same moment I could pray,
And from my neck so free
The Albatross fell off, and sank
Like lead into the sea.

# "NEVER THE SMELL OF THE LAMP"

# — HOMER —
# THE BLIND POET

*Notes*

## SOONER OR LATER

Our poetry lives
As we long think it.
Our poetry dies
Written so soon.

From: *Letters From The Algonquin Hotel*
By: **Alex Blackstone**

*Notes*

# VERITAS

*Notes*

## VERITAS

Poet am I
Resting uneasily beneath my dream
Poet am I
Unknown to you, at times even me


Poet am I
Mind wandering known and unknown worlds
Poet am I
The journey where nothing moves


Poet am I
Failed master of all lost words
Poet am I
Their sounds now master me


Poet am I
Enshrouded with an ultimate truth
Poet am I
Unable to bury the long dead lie

*Notes*

# WORD FRIENDLY

*Notes*

# WORD FRIENDLY

One day late in years
I looked up from this life
And there were only books.

Only they were friends
And yes true lovers too,
Those that never change.

Yet seem to everything change
Even as they match my stare
There upon old shelves waiting.

By a long ago fire's glow,
Those unconditional friends
And unsurpassed lovers.

*Notes*

# NOTHING NEW

When asked by his students:
"O great one, how may one so wise have so many divorces?"

Confucius replied, perhaps smiling, as was his custom upon
the discovery of a perfect answer for an imperfect query.
"Women apparently find it difficult to live with such perfection."

**Confucius**
470 B.C.

*Notes*

## NEVER FORGET

Always keep a journal,
For what is not recorded
Is only as it can be remembered,
Not as it was.

**Alex Blackstone**
Circa 1991

## TRUE FICTION

"Writing fiction is to apply the art of being able
to remember in exact detail all the things that
never happened earlier in your life."

**Alex Blackstone**
Circa 1998

*Notes*

# MUST I BE LIKE ME OR THEE

Your heart says write a novel, create—like F. Scott
Your head refuses, smiles—
"One must have a job."

Your heart says sail the sea, be free—like Joshua Slocum.
Your head refuses, groans—
"One must have a job."

Your heart says learn to fly, soar—like Amelia Earhart
Your head refuses, shudders—
"One must have a job."

Your heart says tramp the globe, explore all—like Joseph Campbell.
Your head refuses, trembles—
"One must have a job."

Your heart says study philosophy, dream—like Socrates.
Your head refuses, gasps—
"One must have a job."

Your heart says be an evangelist, meditate and pray—like Billy Graham.
Your head refuses, frightened—
"One must have a job."

Your heart says be artistic, paint—like Picasso.
Your head refuses, laughs and laughs and laughs—
"One must have a job."

Your heart says try the stage, act—like Helen Mirren.
Your head refuses, scoffs—
"One must have a job—

Your heart says, finally I get it, at last I see—like all the others.
Your head moans and whispers rather sadly—
"Now you're as boring as I."

*Notes*

# UNCONQUERED CONSCIENCE

He always said, almost chanted, that nothing for him came before God, family and Virginia—beautiful, romantic and yes fantastic rationalization for the difficult, grand decision to lead the Confederacy as the sabers rattled from Richmond down to Atlanta. And after all, he'd been well trained at West Point, the heir apparent to lead all the military forces for the greatest young democracy ever, the United States of America.

But after a few early victories, as the rebel yells died hard following the initial crescendos, as power slaughtered enthusiasm, and bravery became a foolish word spoken only by women, or boys who'd never faced a cannon across a naked field, or men who'd never seen a leg amputated in a field hospital, and as the stench of death and horribly infected wounds hung and palled low over the charred battlefields and then floated into even the fine cities of great architecture and culture, the chant began to change and lay trapped within him like a strange leprosy fouling only the insides disguised with a beautiful skin.

Year after year, day after day he marched the gray thousands straight into the sure blue death, as for once we all faced enemies we could not dehumanize. For we faced ourselves, and when he lifted his brain to a higher level of consciousness, as only great men are able, and looked across the lines of the fallen and through the scarlet mist of all the bloody campaigns, he didn't see Grant nor Lincoln or even the cutting edge hordes of Union Blue who'd fought much harder than even he believed they would, but instead saw God, his family and Virginia, and now General Lee dropped his sword to live on yet dead, still breathing, as a man who'd led an army against God's word.

*Notes*

# SYNOPSIS
# UNPUBLISHED POETS

My grandfather remains unpublished, totally out of character. I had to write a book to understand. After all, he'd never avoided the spotlight in any other situation or endeavor, never. And after all, he'd flown with the Lafayette Escadrille against the Red Baron, and earned a law degree from Harvard after marrying into a family of Boston's finest shipbuilders, pretty good credentials for a kid who'd run away from the family farm near Savannah when he was fifteen.

This story takes place in the segregated south in the forties as World War II ends the Holocaust, the victory a great American-European achievement to free a people grown weary of bondage and prejudice. But irony of all ironies, members of the Negro race still languished as second-class citizens even as they cheered the triumphant troops returning home after freeing the Jewish and even as they mourned the dead return of their own coming back to be buried with military honors in graveyards in places continuing to condone separate but equal laws, laws twisting the constitution of the world's greatest democracy and laws compartmentalizing even Christianity's grand plan for Salvation for all mankind.

When I was five I came to live with my grandparents in Ithaca, Georgia, at a time when most smaller southern cities were of two cultures, two proud races dying a torturous death of intolerance. And although America would eventually awaken from this seemingly endless racist coma, the epiphany came much sooner to our otherwise obscure town on the edge of the Okefenokee Swamp, and not as a result of riots, marches, diversification education or even governmental regulations imposed by police or national guardsmen. No, The Game, as it came to be known and will always be remembered, changed everything for us here, our minds and our hearts. Changes so dramatically unbelievable and unexpected I'd originally named this book, The Ithaca Black Senators. For this was a sandlot team they thought could never be, a team that bucked the system to make a difference in the hearts and, yes, souls of all watching them play in 1945.

*Notes*

*Unpublished Poets* begins on a snowy December night outside the Algonquin Hotel in New York in 1920 and ends in the fall of 1945 in Ithaca, Georgia, as a little black kid walks into an all-white school where his father works as a janitor. There were no protests nor hate threats and not one student withdrew from school. The Game made it possible. Now, 1965, not too many of The Game players are still around. But there are always enough to gather once a year and celebrate the end of the separate but equal horror that came very close to destroying our nation of democracy. We don't have to say too much. We look into each others' eyes to see and remember the pain, the glory, the thrill and the truth of 1945, the year the Ithaca Senators and the Ithaca Black Senators played an improbable game, a beautiful game, one perfect game.

In my grandfather's library, after I returned from Korea, I read *A Moveable Feast*, by Ernest Hemingway, the final book of a long list my grandfather had suggested as I'd entered high school. In it, which was his habit, he'd underlined a passage of dialogue. "The truth shall come from unpublished poets." Then he'd noted in the margin, "How would this work as a title for your book?" He meant a book about him, I knew that for sure, but a book about my grandfather would cover a lot of ground, a lot of loves, that's just the way it was with him. So finally I knew what my life was all about, what I would do, but I'd have to write a long time to even come close to understanding it all, and now I realize there is a reason we don't really ever get there, that place where you figure it out, because if you live long enough it just comes to you that the journey is the answer, not the destination.

**Carl Thorpe**
August, 1965
Ithaca, Georgia

*Notes*

# CAPPY'S ANSWERS

What is literature?
>Read Shakespeare.

What is love?
>Read Jesus and Mother Teresa and Shakespeare.

What is hate?
>Read Shakespeare.

What is truth?
>Read Jesus.

What is suffering?
>Read Faulkner.

What is worldly?
>Read Hemingway.

What is political?
>Read Machiavelli and Shakespeare.

What is snobbish?
>Read Fitzgerald.

What is irony?
>Read Wilde.

What is Salvation?
>Read Paul.

What is kind?
>Read Mother Teresa.

What is arrogance?
>Read Custer.

*Notes*

What is warrior?

    Read Geronimo and Crazy Horse.

What is commendable?

    Read *The Lena Baker Story*. By: Lela Bond Phillips

What is oratory?

    Read King and Lincoln.

What is enlightenment?

    Read Voltaire.

What is Yorick?

    Read The Court Jester (Hamlet's surrogate father).

What is solitude?

    Read *Forget Thoreau* and

    read *Sailing Alone Around The World* By: Joshua Slocum, 1844.

What is real?

    Read Wolfe—in a perfect white suit.

What is surreal?

    Read Poe—in an imperfect dark suit.

What is genius?

    Read William F. Buckley Jr.

What is beauty?

    Read The Smile of A Pregnant Woman in the Third Month.

What is courage?

    Read *Night* By: Elie Wiesel.

What is determination?

    Read *The Life of Ida B. Wells*.

What is brilliance?

    Read Ms. Rice Edges Ms. Clinton in Run-Off.

*Notes*

What is Cappy?
    Read—*Unpublished Poets*.

What is compassion / humor?
    Read Vonnegut.

What is talent?
    Read—Vidal, Mailer, Doctorow.

What is complicated?
    Read Umberto Eco.

What is heart / intelligence / tolerance?
    Read / See Oprah.

What is success / writing?
    Read Grisham.

What is perfection?
    Read *Bleachers*.

What is playwright?
    Read Tennessee Williams, David Mamet, Lorraine Hansberry.

What is talent outrageous?
    Read Capote.

What is talent mysterious lovable?
    Read Harper Lee.

What is solid southern terrific?
    Read Rick Bragg.

What is catalyst?
    Read Harriet Beecher Stowe.

What is drama?
    Read Alex Haley.

*Notes*

What is self-published?
> Read *Spartacus* By: Howard Fast

What is life?
> Read Shakespeare.

What is Shakespeare?
> Read Harold Bloom.

What is novella?
> Read Jim Harrison.

What is wild?
> Read *Death In The Long Grass*.

What is biography?
> Read *One Matchless Time* By: Jay Parini.

What is great art, great sadness, great film?
> See *Cobb* By: Ron Shelton

What is wrong?
> Read *Now It's Your Turn*.

What is great resilience?
> Read New Yorkers—9/11!!!

What is necessary?
> Read Support Our Troops— They face death daily for us!!!!

What is ultimate answer?
> Read God.

Why God?
> Read Our Only Chance.

Where is God?
> Read Get On Our Knees—He Will Always Appear, Always.

*Notes*

# GREAT MOMENTS

There just may be a singular, God granted, great moment for us all. When younger, we confuse it and think we know what's coming, what we want to come anyway. Years ago I imagined, often dreamt of, this time, this moment. I envisioned a terrific play high upon a centerfield wall, probably in Brooklyn, a final catch in the seventh game of the World Series. My dad spent many years in the Dodger farm system and our family and most of my friends pulled for them religiously–almost–and waited for the day Big Bobby would be called up from the minors. As the years rolled by we began to wonder, the stats were there and for me, of course, there wasn't any doubt my father was of enough caliber because I'd been the traveling bat boy on a couple of his teams, most notably Anniston, Alabama, the year he'd led the Southeastern League in hitting. He played hard and from the bits and pieces of information a nine year old gets operating below the radar on a baseball team, it was clear he called a good game and the pitchers liked throwing to him. But sometimes I heard the manager curse when some throws bounced by second into centerfield and there were a few times dad sent me down to the hotel lobby for meal money and the manager had a few choice words about why Big Bobby couldn't make it down, why did he have to send me? He knew the answer, we all knew. We also knew that if dad got enough rest before the game we had a good chance of winning that night. I learned very early that winning comes before everything, everything, in pro-fessional baseball. That's why it's so American, I suppose now that I'm older. Anyway, sometimes I had to act hungry and pitiful to convince the manager to give me the two dollar per diem. Once the manager, surrounded by some players hanging out in the lobby, those players that have to do this to stay on the team, told me, "Little Bobby, that's a pretty good act you got there—acting hungry so I'll break my rules and let you have your dad's meal money—maybe you'll turn out to be a movie star instead of a ballplayer." I laughed along with everyone else, but as I passed the reserve catcher, reserve catchers always seem to spend a lot of time hanging out with the manager and laughing at his jokes, good or bad, I said, "When's the last time you got a hit, Byrnes?" I knew he wouldn't retaliate. Dad had a reputation for playing a rough game, on and off

*Notes*

the field. But that night my conscience would get the best of me and I'd just happen to drop by the bullpen and sort of apologize to Byrnes and then Byrnes would make it okay by saying he didn't know what the hell I was talking about, and soon one of the relief pitchers might buy me a hotdog for delivering a note to a lady in the bleachers and everything would be back to normal. That's the way it was with players when they were in uniform, everything was easier, normal, like in baseball everything was reversed from how it was with other ways of making a living.

As I got older and saw both sides of the game, and became more and more influenced by my grandparents with whom I lived after dad returned to the Army to see combat in Korea and Viet Nam, my vision for a great moment to be began to change drastically. I began to think about a prize-winning novel that would not only be a money maker but help those reading it be entertained as well as have a better life. A little far fetched and lofty, but now I know that's the way young ambitious dreams must be to coincide with our high school principal's admonition, "Don't sell yourself short, aim high."

As the years passed those thoughts have not materialized and that's alright as often it's best for some plans to fade to make way for more important ones we might never have dreamed or designed on our own.

For my greatest moment came quietly and unexpectedly a few years ago, and you'll have to admit the years are flying by faster these days, when my father, well over seventy and calmed from all the hard baseball years and strengthened by proving to himself his measure, as many men feel they must, by facing death in battle in wars we must forever truly endure to preserve our freedom—and stock market—walked toward me as never before and put his arm around my shoulders. Dad, now different, calm and detached from all the tests given mankind in this world where constant change really never changes anything human. Big Bobby, finally realizing God is a forgiving taskmaster and really the only one we need ever worry about pleasing, said to me at my lowest personal time, "I understand everything you are going through and I'll do anything to help bring you back and —I love you." And then he walked away, as was his way, but this time was different. He walked away to never really leave me again.

One moment in time, and who would need another? But we must pass it on. For in time we play all roles, in time we are all roles.

# INTERVIEW
## SOUTHERN WRITER'S SERIES
## CIRCA: 2025
## ANDREW COLLEGE
## CUTHBERT, GEORGIA

*Notes*

# MUSINGS PRIOR TO INTERVIEW: CARL THORPE 2025
## MS. MACOMBER'S CREATIVE WRITING 103

Andrew College is a two-year institution established in 1854 and has the unique history of being used as a hospital during the Civil War. Located in sparsely populated southwest Georgia within the city limits of Cuthbert, a small city that has outlived and for the most part survived the infamous racial slur it received in the mid forties when one of its African American citizens, Lena Baker, became the first and only woman to be electrocuted by the state, the once considered small college has grown steadily in the past eighteen years after a movie, *The Lena Baker Story* (A Ralph Wilcox film based upon the scholarly non fiction novel of the same title by Dr. Lela Bond Phillips), gained national recognition for the school originally conceived as a prep setting for university-bound females from the surrounding agrarian area.

Now coeducational and boasting a dramatic increase of more than a thousand students, Andrew has become "the international place to be and study" for budding artistic types, be they writer, painter, musician, actor or even sculptress or sculptor.

Today, I, a novelist with just moderate success anywhere very far from my home of Ithaca, Georgia, and aged eighty seven hard years, am seated before a slightly less than enthusiastic gathering, I notice, of potential writers prepared to endure yet another interview of an author that actually attended this college "back in the day." Fortunately the professor conducting this event for her creative writing class is a young friend of an older friend and has promised to keep things light, and perhaps moderate any over zealous scrutiny form the students, whom all I'm sure surpassed my SAT of twelve hundred scored in antiquity (1955). In these situations, I usually rely on a sense of humor and a worn smile becoming increasingly more difficult to force from behind wrinkles accrued in over eight decades of breathing, and the albatross of my personal adage of never letting the truth get in the way of a good story. It does help I was given a small part in the very movie catapulting their school into national and eventually international prominence. Naturally, I seldom divulge I had only one line in the film which runs for well over two hours in the original version. The line? "Might

*Notes*

be coroner business, John." Some things one never forgets. It was my second movie, mind you. My first was in 1980, *The Long Riders*, a Walter Hill film still the number one rental at Movie Gallery in Dawson, Georgia, maybe because it was filmed in part in Parrott, Georgia, some six miles west of Dawson, maybe not. Anyway, I played the role of a bullet-riddled corpse slung over the swayed back of a horse being led back into the town of Northfield, Minnesota, where the James Gang met their Waterloo, which was why Parrott was chosen as the location since in 1980 it still looked like Northfield had in 1880. But enough about my movie career. Let the interview begin.

*Notes*

# INTERVIEW: ANDREW COLLEGE – 2025

*Ms. Macomber:* "Good morning class. As part of our two thousand twenty five southern writer's series, today we have as our guest, Mr. Carl Thorpe. I first met Mr. Thorpe at Books A Million in Albany during a book signing for his latest novel, *Ain't No Death In Baseball (Just Another League)*, and if you haven't read it, I certainly think you would definitely enjoy it and also it would be very beneficial for our out of state students as the book covers a lengthy time span in south Georgia—from 1938 through 2006. Of course I realize this is a little before your times, but as Mr. Thorpe reiterates in his story, baseball rarely changes and —"

*A male student:* "Neither does Cuthbert."

*Ms. Macomber:* "Tell me about it—don't forget I was born here." One sensed she had excellent rapport with her class.

*Class:* Polite, almost nervous laughter.

*Ms. Macomber:* "Mr. Thorpe got a late start in his writing career, first publishing at the age of forty nine after being in professional baseball the early part of his life after attending Andrew College, Georgia Tech and graduating from West Georgia College. His books, all fiction, include *Largo*, *Twelve Voices*, *Edisontown*, *An Illusion of Victory*, *Letters From The Algonquin Hotel*, *Unpublished Poets* and more recently, *Ain't no Death in Baseball*. As I'm sure you know, the movie rights for *Unpublished Poets* were purchased by Ralph Wilcox Films, Inc. and eventually filmed in 2011 by the same company that did *The Lena Baker Story*, which incidentally was based upon the non-fiction novel of the same name by our very own Dr. Lela Bond Phillips. I've prepared a list of questions for Mr. Thorpe, so, please feel free to record this interview, and, let's see. What have I left—oh yes, please make notes you might need for any questions you have for Mr. Thorpe."

*Class:* Some paper shuffling and a few computers light up. One student exits and mumbles "bathroom" on the way out. I have a feeling she isn't coming back.

*Notes*

*Ms. Macomber:* "Mr. Thorpe, I apologize for not using your complete bio but considering your unique penchant for using multiple noms de plume I felt that by allowing you to more or less provide your own background information—this would be a good intro for you and the class to become more comfortable." Pause. "So, would you mind giving us, shall we say, a quick trip through your life and a few personal feelings about your books. We've read two of your stories from *Legends, Demons and Dreams*, and, oh yes, how many of you have seen the movie *Unpublished Poets*?"

*Class:* A few murmur they have, and about six raise their hands, about half. Then there is that great silence as they stare at you, as Ms. Macomber sits back and takes a deep breath, trying to remember what she just said, if she made any sense at all. I realize interviewing an eighty seven year old writer is not even close to being easy, no matter the agenda, regardless the audience. As my grandfather, a lawyer wannabe poet, advised—"Consider the audience, include the audience, have some fun and above all be brief."

*Carl Thorpe:* "I hope this interview doesn't turn out to be like my sex life. You know, at my age I don't get asked much, and when I do it doesn't last very long. And after it's over I realize I'm the only one got anything out of it."

*Class:* Only moderate laughter. Unusual, because although this joke is an old standard, these are very young people and the odds are they've never heard it, but I notice they are all now staring at the man in the tie. Dr. David Seyle stands in the doorway and I hope and pray he's feigning that grim countenance. My chin drops to my chest as if I have a lead plate in my forehead. But soon the eternal President of Andrew College is smiling and asking Ms. Macomber to be sure and invite me to stay for lunch. When I look up he's gone.

*Carl Thorpe:* "So, that's the punishment I get for telling an off-color joke? The last time I came to Andrew, 2007, I went to the cafeteria to eat and there was a sign on the door—Out to Lunch."

*Class:* Much laughter.

*Ms. Macomber:* Holds up a hand to reset her interview ambience. She carries it off with an expression of—now, class, let's not forget this could be your grandfather here today, or even you someday, if indeed you ever get around to writing your Great American Novel, and always remember, whether you like the

*Notes*

work of an author or not, it is possible you might learn something about the writing life or the art (craft) of creative writing. But she says. "Since this is only day one of our series here of three interviews" she pauses just as several students groan from the rear of the room—"I'd like to first ask Mr. Thorpe about the pen name scenario he discussed with Tom Seegmueller in an article from *Southwest Georgia Living* magazine."

*Carl Thorpe:* "It wasn't planned—not exactly, anyway—It got tricky for me when I found myself hearing three voices. This started abruptly the afternoon in 1988 when my wife and our daughter bravely traveled to St. Simons Island to check me out of alcohol rehab from Charter By The Sea where I'd spent the previous twenty eight days. We stopped in Waycross for lunch and as we ordered, a strange sensation flooded me. They didn't know me. I wasn't the same. It was like I'd been brainwashed (not at all a bad thing, my brain certainly needed a good bath at that time) and in Alcoholics Anonymous they teach us we have to change, because the same man will drink again, and for me at that time and probably even now, to drink again means death, for sure mentally and very likely even physically. So, this sensation shouldn't have really been all that much of a surprise. The surprise came when out of nowhere I said the name, Alex Blackstone. My wife, actress she shall always be, smiled and said, hopefully deterring any confusion in our daughter's mind. 'Someone you met in Charter?' Remember, when I entered rehab I had written only one book, *Largo*, a novel with, according to the one critic actually reviewing it, a 'strong beginning, a vague middle and no ending at all.' This didn't surprise anyone. What did surprise was the book made a profit, aided, I must admit, by several book signings where we held a sort of raffle where people purchasing a book became eligible to win a side by side .410 shotgun, a very popular gun in southwest Georgia, and back then, in the eighties, easily purchased at yard sales for less than a hundred dollars, now they range from five to twenty five thousand. You see, it's all in the pattern. I mean anybody can have success wing shooting, if they have the right choke for their shot gun. Why, I remember----"

*Ms. Macomber:* Taps my shoulder and mercifully (for the students also, I'm sure) hands me a cup of coffee, a prearranged signal I've digressed. A very comforting plan, because if allowed to go too far I have trouble getting back. You just have to know how to handle your flaws, my grandfather used to say. He didn't, actually. It's what I call writer's license, making up something and claiming it was someone else's quote, but then if it catches on, claim it for

*Notes*

yourself. Sort of like that line a pension robbing CEO makes as he also steals a subordinate's fresh idea. "Great idea, I'm glad I thought of it."

*Carl Thorpe:* "Hhmmmmm. Good coffee. Now then, what was the question?"

*Class:* Great amount of laughter.

*Ms. Macomber:* "You were telling us about the first time you were aware of Alex Blackstone, your first—alter ego, I believe you yourself termed it during the Seegmueller article."

*Carl Thorpe:* "Tell you what, let's try another way. You ask each alter ego specific questions. How's that? And really, to tell you the truth, I'd feel more comfortable if they were known as maybe—inner voices."

*Ms. Macomber:* "Fine." She looks at her watch.

*Class:* They look at their watches—or rather the time shown on their cell phones. One female student inadvertently turns on her cell phone. A weird space voice, I guess you'd call it, immediately drones— "Call Ronnie. Call Pete. Call Ross. Call Mike. Call Milt. Call Paul. Call—" She finally finds the off button.

*Male student:* "Damn, Janelle, just call the whole Falcon football team!"

*Janelle:* Waits until Ms. Macomber looks down at some notes, then gives the jokester what we used to call a "California howdy" or a "We're number one" sign. I'm not sure I want to know what it's called now in 2025.

*Ms. Macomber:* "Okay. Let's start with Alex Blackstone."

*Carl Thorpe:* "Very aggressive, impossible to embarrass, sort of all the things I could be when I was drinking, but Alex doesn't have to drink. If a choice had to be made in a sentence whether to have the character curse or not, Alex would always go for the vulgarity, the vulgarity I knew was true to the dialogue but I worried what people would think of me or my family if that kind of language showed up in the book. That kind of thinking really kills a writer, really smothers him—her." I glance at Ms. Macomber. She pats her hands lightly together as if applauding. I continue. "Some people curse. If you write about a person that curses and he says something in your story and you've lived in your mind day

*Notes*

in and day out with him, or her," I glance again but Ms Macomber has turned the page and is planning the next question and doesn't applaud— "Then to be true to your work, you must use the profanity. And it isn't to be commercial, because there are many writers with very lucrative careers that seldom if ever use obscenities. Until Alex Blackstone barged in, neither did I, and I didn't enjoy writing until his voice convinced me I had to write true to what I know. For instance, when a three hundred and fifty thousand dollar Rolls Royce fails to start for a rap star as he's leaving awards night in front of the Four Seasons Hotel, I ain't no Nostradamus but I think he's probably going to say, 'Why you --------!!!'"

*Class:* Very, very much laughter!! Then once again that great silence you come to dread but learn to live with when you use off-the-wall humor.

*Ms. Macomber:* Looks at her notes, but even in that position I detect a forced archaic smile as if upon Greek sculpture.

*Carl Thorpe:* "What I mean is—I think the toughest point to come to is where you write what you want to write and not what you think the publishers want. Most writers, and I mean people with some very noble aspirations—after those first rejections, well, bow to commercialism. Same old thing, Heller's Catch 22. It's very romantic, of course, to be a struggling writer in New York or Paris and go to bars at night or outdoor cafes and hold court claiming you only write to express your art, and that, according to Hemingway, only unpublished poets give us the truth. But even he finally gave in as one of his characters in *A Moveable Feast* mused 'Of course, there is the problem of sustenance.' Like, where's the grocery and rent money coming from? Of course now, we're talking fiction writers, not journalism nor how-to writers, nor self-helpers. All very fine and all reliable ways of making sure your family gets a check now and then, but for me it's all about the books that help people forget about how much crap they had to take at work, or how they're going to pay the taxes the rich people have figured out how to make ordinary Joe pay while they flourish behind complicated deductions created by faceless corporations of the invisible empire operating and ruling far above and beyond the White House and its cast of face lifted, dyed hair, or wigged puppets answering only to laws they create themselves for themselves, or forget about why your kids have to sign their lives away for college loans while other kids get scholarships because their dads were in the same fraternity with the guys handing out the free passes, or forget about how bad it feels to work a lifetime at some place like Enron only to discover you don't get your pension because some low-life CEO scammed all the funds so he could

*Notes*

hang a Degas on his wall in a penthouse on Fifth Avenue, or forget that rich people start wars, middle class people pay for them and poor people fight and die trying to win them. To me, fiction is to entertain and if you've lived life long enough, and I'm talking about life in the real world where you have to get up early and scuffle until dark to make it or get what you want or be what you want to be, you'll probably pass on a little something now and then within your stories to help somebody have a better life, or, maybe you'll be as good as Pat Conroy and take people places with your work, places they didn't even want to go or never thought about going. Take us to another level, guide us to deeper, even subliminal thinking, out of ourselves, like a space flight so surreal you completely forget you're in a simulator, beyond the stars, beyond dreams, beyond all boundaries, thousands of hours of discovery with absolutely no risk, where we go without fear or expectation, where one image, one sentence or even one word can change our mindsets, our lives—and what about that last passage in *The Great Gatsby*—'Gatsby believed in the green light, the orgastic future that year by year recedes before us. It eluded us then, but that's no matter—tomorrow we will run faster, stretch out our arms farther—and one fine morning—So we beat on, boats against the current, borne back ceaselessly into the past.' And Faulkner saying a family heirloom, a pocket watch, was 'the mausoleum of all hope and desire,' so perfect, and Hemingway always knowing precisely what to put in and precisely what to leave out and having written so well we understand and know all the blank spaces, their emptiness somehow filling the lonely holes in us all. Robert Penn Warren walking Jack out of the old mansion 'into the convulsion of the world, out of history into history and the awful responsibility of Time.' It's two A.M., alarm set for seven, but you sit there and stare at page six sixty one, hold the book in your hand, amazed at the power so greatly described by Voltaire, remembering that a good book helps you sleep while a great one won't let you. And so grandeur, Shakespeare's Joan of Arc's, 'Glory is like a circle in the water which never ceaseth to enlarge itself till by broad spreading it disperse to naught.' Then Nobel Prize-winning Toni Morrison's stunning conclusion to, *Sula*. 'It was a fine cry—loud and long—but it had no bottom and it had no top, just circles and circles of sorrow.' And the genius of Arthur Miller's *The Crucible*, a grand play of satan using fanatical sacredness and superstition to imprison the souls of the very men founding America to be free to worship as they pleased. Great drama, great prose, great art, great history (and never forget—Arthur was married to Marilyn Monroe—just in case you think all writers lead dull lives). And last and at last, Henry, creator of fantastic verbosity, Miller, clear mostly to the border-line insane, truly troubled, self proclaimed misunderstood Oscar Wilde wannabes ruling a nebulous rhetorical

*Notes*

fantasyland where sound, irony and arrogance conquer content and hope until there is no reason for anything anywhere and inner peace comes only with the reaper—until you read it long enough and live it long enough to hear God laugh as evil plays inevitably right into His hands. Words and phrases, characters leaving their creators in the dust, traveling alone, masters of their masters, like for instance prize-winning novelist Cormac McCarthy, a fiction writer with descriptive powers so powerful we are perfectly transported across and beyond all literary borders but literally below the Mexican-American border where the world is 'beautiful and desolate, rugged and cruelly civilized.' A world where one may be brutally poor or rich and arrogant, but rarely in the middle, no, never the middle, nothing is rare there in the middle, and there is no deception, the lines aren't blurred, lines drawn hard and held fast for centuries, years so hesitant to make way for new years of progressive change. Old dreamers holding on hard with war-bloodied, intolerant-bloodied, economic-bloodied hands, holding all new dreamers hostage until they are suspended, suspended within lives of no consequence, left alone to die wondering if it is all good or bad or neither.

Yet beyond McCarthy's stunning, stirring, haunting prose and descriptive greatness and uncannily true bilingual dialogue we find ourselves moved across still another border into a new 'not-always-safe' land of broken rules of literary tradition and literary convention, a new place of ingeniously created semantics, narrative, juxtaposition, and disguised poetry, a new place where a few words or phrases may total a lifetime of contemplation, meditation, intro-spection, retrospection, and vision. For example, from *All The Pretty Horses*, (written years before *No Country For Old Men*) this superbly Shakespearean, Faulknerean, internalization by a young cowboy who has been rejected for all the wrong reasons by an older, elegant lover, a lady from another country, another class, 'He saw very clearly how all his life led only to this moment and all after led nowhere at all. He felt something cold and soulless enter into him like another being, and he imagined that it smiled malignly and he had no reason to believe that it would ever leave.' Stunning, stirring, haunting, timeless.

And it is difficult to praise McCarthy and not move on to Michael Ondaajte, particularly to his novel *Divisadero*, where he totaled the price for all cursed and blessed with an inordinate, inexplicable desire to write.

'"When I wrote," the man said, "that was the only time I would think. I would sit down with a notebook and a pen, and I would be lost in a story." The old writer, seemingly at peace, thus casually suggested to Rafael, a path he might take during his own life, and taught him how he could be alone and content, guarded from all he knew, even those he loved, and in this strange way, be fully understanding of them. It was in a sense a terrible proposal of secrecy,

*Notes*

what you might do with a life, with all those hours being separated from it that could lead somehow to intimacy. The man had made himself an example of it. The solitary in his busy and crowded world of invention. It was one of the last things he talked to him about.'

*Ms. Macomber:* "Mr. Thorpe. Mr. Thorpe?" She looks at her watch and smiles, spreads her hands as if apologizing that our first session has ended, but the smile is not now archaic. Not at all, only the sincere expression of an intelligent, literary smitten, young lady with compassion for an old man lost in his passion for the written word. And of course I understand as the students bolt for the door, some of them. Several stop by and say they look forward to tomorrow, even wait long enough to laugh as I tell them I hope I'll make it, because just this morning when I ordered two-minute eggs at the Huddle House the waitress made me pay in advance. I thank them for enduring an old man's ramblings, tell them I know I need to upgrade my examples and I promise tomorrow I'll do just that as tonight I plan to reread John Grisham's *Bleachers*, or Conroy's greatest latest, *Charleston Midnights*, and they slide away to the door and I look at the empty chairs. The only thing worse would be a small coffin, as here we think of Jim Harrison's words, or that stiff dead hand protruding from a mangled, frozen pile of corpses in Korea, imagery forever to haunt Rick Bragg's father as he stared into the bottle that became his family. At once all so ugly and beautiful, so timeless. And maybe Picasso was right, maybe all writers would rather paint, as now I think again of Van Gogh's paintings of empty chairs in his bleak room, a powerful revelation of how much he cared for people gone, no longer ever to return until all that is left to love is the emptiness of rejection. Could a writer make that much of a chair? Capote, Tennessee Williams, David Mamet, Wolfe, Poe, Steinbeck, Uris, Hughes, King, Wharton, Cather, Vonnegut, Crane, Angelou, Morrison, Oates, Wilde, McCullers, Eugene O'Neil, Rand, Welty, Flannery O'Connor, Harper Lee, Reynolds Price. They did everything else, why not make a chair breathe, have a heartbeat, a voice, anything and all things. Now I wonder why I never say this at the right moment. Aahhh, that vast mysterious chasm between think a thing and say—Soon I'm just staring into the "midspace" Vidal made so famous, or was it Mailer? Don't you just love the fireworks when they are on the same talk show? Now a thick silence moves in, an early morning fog, and it's difficult to see even right in front of you, but you put out a hand through it, hoping, searching for the right word or phrase, finally realizing Hemingway was always out front, knowing, passing it all along, "What's true at first light is a lie by noon." And there is no way I cannot think here of the man in the perfectly perfect white suit existing out there somewhere with his laser-like fiction,

*Notes*

sliding along above all levels with every phrase a rebellion and a creation. Tom Wolfe, master of, *Bonfire of The Vanities*, *A Man In Full*, and, *I Am Charlotte Simmons*, a genius of the written word gleaned from almost supernatural observation with surgically precise, savage (ironically beautiful) attacks upon our lives, personalities, mores, beliefs and languages, able to critically recognize, compartmentalize, expose and yes humiliate all things merely human, his words slapping our faces with, with—us, but with such artistry we bow to the preeminence and as if from a trance find ourselves praying (in private mind you—especially we of Atlanta and Baker County, Georgia) he never turns it all upon himself, for no degree of payback should hold that horror.

We hear you, also, Mr. E.L. Doctorow, we of the South and all those from history starting wars for reasons not noble enough to have started wars, we hear you from, *The March*, "He could see the grand statehouse the city fathers had been attending, a handsome, half-finished classical structure in granite. Very appropriate to a community that thought so well of itself. With what a sense of security they must have kept abreast of the war up North. To be author of it and yet be safe from it."

*Ms. Macomber:* Her eyes appear to tear. But she's a woman and when she faces me they're dry. I never did understand how they do that. She says, so softly, as if she doesn't want to disturb those literary ghosts only some can see and hear. "I think they really got something here today, Mr. Thorpe." She trails the sentence—probably wondering why I didn't mention Maya Angelou more, or the mysterious Emily Barrett, or Patty Rasmussen's new blockbuster, or Paul Hemphill's *Oeuvre*. She has a far-away look, wondering what it is book people share, someday she'll understand we really don't have to understand it, like religion, all we have to do is enjoy the inner peace of it. Never intellectualize worship and never worship intellect. Maybe Harold Bloom said it, maybe not. Or, what about Dylan's *Chronicles*, maybe there? Now I've got Harold Bloom and Bob Dylan on the same page. I don't think either will mind. Great art transcends education. I do recall Bob Dylan saying New Orleans is like a great long poem.

*Carl Thorpe:* "You and your students are very kind, but I think I probably should go on over to Darton. I promised O. Vic I'd try to get there early so we can make some plans for his literary festival next month. Can you believe he's still teaching—after that huge success with the novel, *Costa Rican Lovers*.

*Ms. Macomber:* "Maybe he just loves writing as much as we love writing?"

*Carl Thorpe:* I nod gratefully at this, the ultimate compliment at the end of the day. But I also notice she doesn't try to talk me into coming back for the next two sessions. That's happening more and more these days. "I wonder what that means for us?" Says I (Carl Thorpe). "Who cares?" Says he (Alex Blackstone). "We'd better be grateful we had one day." Says me (Bobby Dews). Says I, says he, says me. The students were lucky today. They only had to listen forty minutes. I'm with me twenty-four seven, three sixty five. However, I never complain, considering the alternative.

Ms. Macomber and I walk to the cafeteria. I can't believe how many people there are on campus. I slow my pace even more at the thought of the noise inside, of all the faces I'm supposed to remember. I get that heavy feeling in my chest, breathe deeply, almost a sigh, but the young literature teacher reaches over and holds my hand, shares her courage and strength, and once again I'm at it again with all those plots and characters vying for attention in my old brain, and tonight the phone might ring and my new book might have a publisher, and then I'll know everything will be alright, and if it isn't—I'll write it until it is.

**THE END**

Made in the USA
Charleston, SC
15 January 2010